MARIOTA

In the New Nation, forged by Robert the Bruce and tempered by chilling assaults through its southern marches, the Wolf of Badenoch burned his way into Scottish history. He plundered the Church, defied his royal father, and loved, beyond life, his spirited, beautiful mistress, Mariota de Athyn. In her early teens she learned the craft of love in the beds of two kings, and understood the unrelenting need to fight with her wits for what she had, or wanted. She was content to leave her family of boys to the whims of their wild father, who tested them in the arts of combat necessary to their lawless lives. She controlled her households at Ruthven, Lochaneilean and Lochindorb with feminine artistry, and her admirers, with the savage grace of a wild cat. She played with their emotions, and seduced their thoughts, briefly, from pillage and war. But with one, it was not a game.

By the same author
The Wolf
Blood of the Wolf

Mariota – First Published in Great Britain 1981 by Robert Hale,
London (ISBN 0-7091-8877-3)

This edition published in 2003 by

Librario Publishing Ltd

ISBN: 1-904440-33-9

Copies can be ordered via the Internet
www.librario.com

or from:

Brough House, Milton Brodie, Kinloss
Moray IV36 2UA
Tel /Fax No 00 44 (0)1343 850 617

Printed by 4edge Ltd, Hockley. www.4edge.co.uk

MARIOTA

CHARLES MACKIE

Librario

Prologue

John Hamilton, archivist and antiquary, sat on the arm of his leather chair. His eyes, watching me over steel half-glasses, were wrinkled at the corners by a mixture of amusement and excitement. My wet anorak hung darkly over the back of the couch and my lower half was steaming in the warmth of the fire at my back. He thrust a tumbler of pale sherry at me.

"You're in the civilised half of Scotland now and I don't spend good money on government tax for the highland rot-gut you distil up north in your tundra. This has hot Spanish sun in it and the slim ankles of the senoritas of Jerez." John Hamilton walks with a limp, the legacy of hard tackling that a stand-off-half accepts during his rugby career. We had made the noises, more or less polite, that two men make when they meet after a long time. He had asked when my wife was going to leave me and come and look after him and I had responded that with his reputation I would soon have to lock up my daughters. In the lull that ended the courtesies, I could see him waiting for the question I was bound to ask. He was balanced on his metatarsals just as I remembered him in the old days, waiting for that ball from the base of the scrum. Like a good number eight I held it just a little longer. It wasn't easy. The question had been on my lips since I left Elgin and it was the anticipation of an answer that had sped me over the Grampians between high walls of ploughed snow.

"Well what have you found?" I could delay the question no longer. John Hamilton caught the ball and side-stepped. He offered me a cigar and then pulled out his tobacco pouch.

"What would you say if I told you that Mariota was a whore?" He was watching me as he rubbed his filling and packed his pipe and laughed outright when he saw my face.

"Don't tell me you swallowed Philip Hogeston's story? All that guff about the gentle mistress of Lochindorb?"

I tried to be flippant. "Be careful Hamilton, you are talking of the woman I love."

He chuckled. "I was aware of that, my bonny man. And if she captured your sentimental heart how many others do you think have fallen for her shining eyes, her husky voice and her small hot hands?" Hamilton lifted a cube of peat and laid it gently on the embers. Then he picked up the La Ina and slushed its pale liquid into our two glasses. He had me by the short and curlies. He knew it and he was enjoying it. In the old days he had used this same technique at the Tower Hotel before launching into one of his long lascivious stories. As I watched him I could feel again the keen expectant hush from twenty-nine sweaty players as they hung on his every action and nuance. He bent over a cabinet and pulled out a drawer. "I have here," he murmured, "the evidence of one of Mariota's closest acquaintances, female."

He lifted out a red folder and handed it to me. Pasted on the outside was a label and on it he had written:

"The testimony of Hilda McDonnell of Auchtertipper, maid and mistress of robes to Mariota de Athyn, concubine of The Wolf of Badenoch." I opened the folder. The first paragraph was on old and faded vellum and I recognised the square firm script of John Winchester, Bishop of Elgin Cathedral in the Province of Moray until his death in 1466. I knew it well. The deposition began, "I Hilda McDonnell, now McInnes, being of sound mind and before witnesses, swear by The Grail that what I now describe is the true history of certain events told to me or witnessed by me during my association with Mariota de Athyn and Alexander Stewart, Earl of Buchan and Badenoch. I swear by the Blood of Jesus that I tell of these matters to Bishop Winchester of my own free will and without coercion or duress."

Thereafter Hamilton had copied the deposition, which plainly had taken the form of cross-examination, conforming to a plan which must have been prearranged by the bishop for clarity and ease of recapitulation, having much in common with the summary of evidence in an advocate's brief for defence or for prosecution. I scanned the first few pages and looked at the thickness of the folder. In volume, the testimony must have exceeded eighty thousand words. "You may take this away with you, Mac. The original is too frail and too valuable to leave the archives, even to photo-copy, which is why I have so laboriously produced it in manuscript."

I spent that night with him. He had arranged a dinner party. The meal was prepared and served by his bidey-in. He considers marriage a dismal institution since his wife died some years ago and his family have flown the nest, and, at intervals, invites various females to live with him on a temporary or holiday basis. All have been successful exponents of 'women's rights'. For instance I can recollect a dressmaker, a lawyer, an ordained minister of the Church of Scotland. They all had in common an expertise in home cooking and a fondness for John Hamilton — never, I believe, a passion — but a warm tenderness to which he responds, like a domesticated cat, with huge purrs of contentment. His guests that night were an exciseman, a director of social work and a chief inspector of police. After dinner we began the evening with liar-dice and ended a poker-school in the wee sma' hours. His hostess of the moment was a very good-looking nursing sister from Grantown on Spey. We had suggested to her that she make it strip poker but, out of consideration, she said, for our inebriation and therefore lack of libido, she refused. The exciseman, an R.N.V.R. navigator in the last war, broke into song and our offended sexuality was soon forgotten when she gave an erotic impersonation of a striptease artist and was carried on our shoulders around the room to the tune and words of "The Ball of Kirriemuir".

Weeks later, when I was working through the confession of Hilda, I remembered that evening at Hamilton's place. Six centuries hung between Mariota de Athyn, The Wolf of Badenoch, and me. In the passage of time, what is done by men and by women, and what they say, is altered by something that we call civilisation, which, like a veneer on our true selves, adorns us as the water-lily adorns the summer face of a highland loch. Yet, however pretty the loch may then look, it is still deep, still dangerous. Men have not changed, I thought, nor women either. Cut us and we bleed. Undress us, and behold the willing Adam and the wanton Eve.

One

The girl and her nurse fled along a track sunk deep in willow-herb and nettles. The girl had lost her shoes in the mud and her legs bled from thorns that snared her young ankles. Her nurse, a youngster of seventeen, snivelled and complained and was tugged on at a fast stumble by her charge.

"Oh damn you, Bertha, do pull yourself together and hurry," the child cried and her voice was breathless, tearful and angry. "You know the men will search for me and you know where your master told us to go. Come on."

They ran on down the dark tunnel of trees, branches flicking their cheeks, towards an oval of pink, sunset sky. Behind them were the horrid roar and crackle of the burning castle, the hoarse shouts of men and the bellowing of frightened cattle. The drove path was recently fouled by the stinking turds of beasts, hurriedly whipped from their byre, that now lowed in terror in the blazing fortress. "I canna go on mistress," wailed Bertha, "I'm caught in brambles. Let me die. I want to die."

The child spun round and tore at the thorns with her own hands. "You're not going to die Bertha. I won't let you. You've got to come with me. I can't go alone. I need you, Bertha. Hurry please." Bertha wiped her wet nose with her sleeve, wrenched her woollen skirt from the thorns and gripped the girl's cold hand. "All right my dear, all right, my dear. Bertha will bide wi' you."

The two girls splashed on down the lane then out on to the mown fields. Behind them flames blazed high from the upper windows of the castle. There was a crash and a woomph as the wooden roof fell in. Hill, valley and woods were lit by the cloud of rising sparks. Cheers came from men, on horse and foot, who stood back from the inferno, shouting "To hell with the traitors. To hell with Baliol. Roast Athyn!

9

Roast with your fat Fife cattle!" The sharp stench of burning hide, evoking primitive emotions, quickened their blood and swelled their loins.

"They will scorch and burn as well without us. We'll have the women." The speaker raised his sword in mock salute to the flames. "I'll see you in hell, Sir Athyn. Put in a good word for me with the Devil. Tell him to expect Alexander Stewart at his gates when my time is ripe. Tell him to look out for cousin King David any day noo — not on horseback but astride his hoor Margaret Drummond." The other men laughed, but one, plainly a leader and a noble, called out:

"Hold your tongue, Alexander. We butcher traitors but do not quarrel with the King."

"Aye, brother Walter," came the quick retort, "but when the King talks surrender to Edward of England and offers his throne to a Plantagenet Pup then the King betrays Scotland and quarrels with me! Come, men, let's catch the quines. De Athyn had five saucy dochters and a wife not much older than yourself, Walter. You can have her if you can find her. Search the woods, but ca canny, for like enough their master will have sent them an escort. Finders keepers and a good tumble to you all."

Dawn came. Curled in each other's arms, the two girls lay inside a cole of hay in a field five miles from the castle. They had not expected to walk so far but the raiders had lifted the hay-cocks nearby and set them alight against the castle gates. The youngest of the girls wriggled her head and shoulders free of the straw and pulled some of the tickling stalks from her bodice. Dawn coloured the tops of the Lomonds. The sun flashed on Loch Leven and dew glistened on the hedges and bent each blade of grass under a silver load. She looked for the castle and tears spilled down her cheeks when she caught sight of its smoking ruin. Her father, two of her brothers and all the remaining men must have perished. Thank God her mother and her sisters by now would be at Portmoak safe in the hospice with Brother Gregory. Poor papa! When he sent his ladies under escort to safety he must have known he had made the defence of his castle impossible. It was already weak when Matthew rode off to the King's Court and took six good men with him. How long ago was that? Goodness, today was Friday and Matthew had left on Wednesday. Papa had not thought he could be attacked so soon by such a force. She twisted in the hay and prodded her companion with her foot. "Bertha, rouse yourself. Bertha, wake up, you sluggard." Her nurse gave a wail. "Stop blubbering," commanded her charge. "What a baby you are! What do you think has happened to mother and the others? Do you think they have escaped?"

"Of course they escaped," sniffled Bertha. "And we would be with them safe in Portmoak now if you hadn't been so busy killing off your dolls. Look at us now, alone, wet and hiding in a hayrick when we could be with Lady Margaret and your sisters, safe and warm." The girl turned and stared coldly at her nurse. "I couldn't leave Penelope and Phoebe and Black Boy in the nursery at the mercy of these cruel people, could I? If we had been murdered what would they, poor things, have done without me? God will put their heads back on in heaven!" There was a renewed howling from Bertha until suddenly the girl said, "Ssht. They are coming! Keep quiet, Bertha, or you will end up in heaven too, on the end of a pikestaff!" Their hearts beating fast, the two girls wriggled into the hay. Over the meadow rode a troop of horse, harness jingling, voices growing louder. When they were level with the row of hay-coles one of them said, "Woa lass," then, "Who's for a piss?" Saddles creaked and feet thumped on the earth. Bertha covered her eyes and her ears. Her companion peeped through the thin screen of drying grass. All she could see was a pair of booted legs of a man urinating on the straw. "Ha! Look at young Will," said the first voice. "Forked-piss Armstrong!" The others laughed. Big hands fastened the trousers and the man beside the rick retorted, "It stopped Bess from crying for her mother so it's nae that bad."

From the haycock came a cry. The girl tumbled out, got to her feet and tore with her hands at the man called Will Armstrong. "You vile brute! she screamed. "Bess is my sister."

"Steady, steady girl," said the astonished young man, warding off the small fists that battered at him.

"What have you done to Bess and mother and all of them, you wicked, wicked men?' She found herself in the centre of a group of twenty soldiers all of them as astonished as young Will Armstrong was, at her spectacular appearance.

"Stop it, woman," shouted Armstrong, a hand up to his scratched face. "Bess is well enough. Damn it, she quite liked it at the end." There was a wail from inside the hayrick.

"God's truth! Twa o' them!" The man with an osprey feather in his cap said, "Look out lads! Here's another bonxie!"

Bertha wriggled out of the heap of straw and the men retreated in mock alarm. Anything less like an attacking skua it was hard to imagine; bedraggled, her long woollen skirt hitched up under her belt, her plump legs searched for the ground.

"Come awa, mistress," said the man who seemed to be the leader. "Tak' the straw frae your lugs and let's have a look at ye. Christ! but you're nae at your best the morn!"

"Let her alone," shouted her companion. "Kill me if you must, but Bertha's a simple skivvy lass with nae mair brains than a hen."

"Well, well," said the man. "So we've caught another of Athyn's clutch. And what, mamselle, is your name?" The girl, straight and pink as a mountain ash, stared at him.

"I am Mariota de Athyn," she said, "And who are you?" The man doffed his bonnet. "I am Alexander Stewart, at your command." He mocked her but she returned his look. As haughtily as she knew how she said, "Take me to your master, Stewart. I do not speak with lackeys!" There was a gust of laughter from the other men. Stewart's long bearded face showed annoyance and admiration.

"I am my own master, young madam. I am Alexander, son of the Regent Robbie." A quick glance warned his men that only he could speak so flippantly of his father the Earl. The red-faced girl with the haughty eyes stood stiffly in front of him. He saw the straw in her flaxen hair and dirty feet below her scratched legs. He admired her nipped waist below her tiny breasts.

"Mamselle de Athyn," he said quietly. "Your father is burned with his castle. So shall end all traitors to Scotland."

Mariota rushed at him and Stewart caught her by her wrists.

"You dare to repeat that slander," she shouted at him. "Then before God and these cowards I swear to kill you. Never was a de Athyn a traitor. My family has been loyal to Scotland as long as de Bruce. You, a mere Stewart, dare accuse a de Athyn of treachery!"

"My God, madam, had you been a man you would be dead."

"I wish then I was a man. Better dead than despoiled by the likes of you. Where have you left my poor mother and my sisters? Do they lie in their blood with their legs tied open? Call yourselves men!" She swung round on the others of the troop. "If you have a spark of manliness or chivalry in you you will take me to the hospice at Portmoak where my mother and my sisters should be by now, were it not for your — diversions!'

Alexander Stewart stared at her. For once in his life he had nothing to say. He mounted his horse.

"Mackay," he called out to one of his soldiers.

"We shall do as this lady says. Lift her up on to the saddle behind me and take you the other wench on your horse's back. Now, you whoremongers, search out the women you lay with last night and kindly, mark you, kindly, offer them your escort to the Hospice of Portmoak."

Two

The King spat into the fire and turned to face the two by the bed, his fleshy, angry face as red as his woollen night-shirt. Nothing had been said since he entered the room. The girl peeped over the bedcovers and the man stood, naked to his knees. Then the King's bearded face split open to snow broken teeth and he laughed. "Upon my soul, Robert, don't you think you are a bit long in the tooth for this sort of caper! You look like a granddad caught robbing his granddaughter's money-box — an apt description, don't you think?" He looked at the girl, her eyes wide open above the furs. "How old are you, child?"

She giggled and answered all pert and sweetness. "Old enough, sire, as you know."

Her companion made to cover his nakedness. "Stand still, Robert. I enjoy your predicament too much to end this charade. Stay there, I say, or I shall open the door and shout for Elizabeth. Look at him, girl. Does that old object turn you on, that grasshopper, when you have known the horn of a real man?" The King turned to his nephew. "So this is the protection you provide for your ward, Robert!

For this, was it, you set your bastard sons loose on poor de Athyn. Do you 'protect' the mother so cosily as you protect her daughter or, in your dotage, is your fancy only for wee quines? Yes, in your dotage, Robert, for, my God, you look your age. I am eight years younger, and lustier than you, Regent Robbie, but you look more like my grandfather!" He strutted across the room and viewed his victim again.

"By the whores of Jerusalem I relish this moment, my proud scorn-faced nephew. Where is your condescension now! Speechless? You were ever quick to taunt and sermonise your King in public. Does the presence of this whorelet tie your tongue? Are you afraid I may subpoena her as witness! Heir to the throne indeed! You compelled me to name you — you and the Douglas — but I scarce thought my luck would change as fast. I have you by the short hairs now, my fine mannie. Aye, thanks to her, I can redress the balance and name my successor in my own good time. And that may not be long delayed since Margaret Logie thinks she is now pregnant. But, my Christ, I've enjoyed this more than whoring. Go to it, Regent Robbie, heir to the throne that was. Have your pleasure. It could be your last." The King laughed. "If you can be upstanding now you're a better man than I took you for!" He ringed a finger in a carnal gesture and left the room.

The girl giggled. "Go to it then, my lord," she mimicked, her cheeky face all innocence. Robert Stewart glared at her, grabbed his cloak and followed the King out of her chamber.

Mariota drew up her long legs under her buttocks and let the fur wrap fall below her hips. She studied her shoulders, her plump breasts and her boyish thighs. She ran the pink tip of her tongue between the small gap in her front teeth and smiled, dimples winking on either cheek. "How flattering." she mused, "to have a King, and perhaps a future King, lusting for me! More exciting if they had been younger men." She thought, "I am grateful to Robert for giving me a home and I am sorry for David with his barren women." She could not remember his first Queen, but palace gossip had made her out to be a stiff and haughty woman, who rated her royal English ancestry higher than her position as Queen of Scotland. Mariota knew all about the King's mistresses and shivered when she remembered the fate of Kathleen Martime, murdered, and with the tacit approval of Queen Joan. Margaret Drummond, Lady Logie, had been luckier. The Queen had died before she had got word of that affair and the Drummond woman had slipped easily into her place in the royal bed. She was no better than she looked, an ambitious whore who dreamed now of nothing but to be filled with child by the King. Mariota frowned and pulled her knees up to her chin. Here was a great mystery. Margaret Drummond said she was now pregnant and yet her mistress of the robes had whispered to the other women in attendance that the Queen's womb was full of wind and that her pregnancy was nothing but hope and longing. How could this be, thought Mariota, when her monthlies had stopped and her belly was growing. Was it possible for a woman to go through all the misery of early pregnancy and yet be barren? She had to ask her mother. It seemed incredible. And meanwhile the King makes this his excuse for tumbling me in bed! Men are so predictable and some women so hard to understand. What of myself? Am I to be used by these two to further their ambitions? She knew what would happen now. Her daddy-man, Robert, would have no more of her. She could picture his stony, humourless face tomorrow. But the King was past caring with whom he shared his pleasures and would be back for more. And, as surely, Margaret Drummond — few could really think of her as Queen — would learn of his infidelity. Robert would see to that. Mariota shivered again. She had seen a pretty girl's face scarred by a jealous woman's nails. She sat up. "I must get me a protector," she said aloud. "But who?" Even as she spoke she knew who it must be. He was tall, strong, feared by his friends and even by his family. She pulled the furs around her, closed her eyes and thought hard about Alexander Stewart.

Three

Mariota dreamed. As dawn paled the sky and the black-birds poured their joyous cadenzas from the roof corners, she awoke to the clamour of their song and willed her dreams to come true. Light slowly peeked through her little window and her face, from a ghostly blur in her silver mirror, became clear. She smiled and saw her small, spaced teeth shine back at her and the faint shadow of the two dimples below the arch of her cheeks. She combed her hair, wrestling with the tugs until the fine pale threads flowed from the top of her head to her collar-bones. Carefully she parted them and with a small knife cut a long tress from where she thought its loss would not easily be seen. By now the night-cap clouds on the Pentlands were wearing their sparkling crown of morning and in her little room high above the-courtyard she worked steadily on the lock of hair, pleating and folding it into a heart-shaped love-knot. She went to her closet where her clothes hung, unfastened a small silver brooch from her cloak and threaded the hair-heart on to the pin. She slipped a gown on her shoulders, tied it round her waist and left the room.

The house was dark and silent. Down corridors and stairs she moved, like a ghost, until she came to the hall where the men lay snoring. She leaned against the wall and looked for Alexander among the sleeping shapes. The stink of sour mead and stale beer made her wrinkle her nose. A cask of ale dripped lees on the floor and stoups and tankards lay tumbled among snoring men or sat on the long table like headless gnomes. She lifted her gown and stepped daintily over legs and bodies until she came to the one she sought. He lay on his back, head pillowed on a leather jacket, stockinged feet with toes poking through, resting on his riding-boots; a handsome bearded man whose face was softened by sleep. His lips were parted and he looked younger and vulnerable than by day when he wore his mask of wariness. She bent over him and gently pinned the love-heart to his shirt. She stood up, brushed her long pale hair from her eyes, smiled at the sleeping man and tiptoed from the hall.

Back on her couch she cuddled the furs closely round her and thought of the man sleeping below. She screwed her eyes tight shut and willed her desire into his sleeping head. "Remember me. Dream of me. Come to me." Her body trembled. She tightened her eyes until small lights flashed inside her head and sweat welled from her skin. She was winning. Her hands, her legs, her stomach, her face, her graceful young body floated on pillows of warm contentment. She had willed him to dream of her, willed the longings that she had woven into the strands of her hair, to reach his heart. She sighed and slid into down-soft sleep.

Four

Two men sat in a small room, hugging the hearth. Outside, a wet nor'-easter puffed gustily against the castle rock and, from the dark, rain spattered on their small window like giant's spit. The bigger of the two men rocked a tankard and watched the head form on its amber wine.

"I'll tell you. I was there and can remember every word spoken. The Regent was seated across the table from me — as you are now and about as far away. Platefuls of excellent meat pie, steaming hot, were being ladled out.

The conversation was thin and I remember thinking that, with all the wine we had drunk, someone should be saying something. Then the Regent shouted down the board at his son. 'Alexander. How serious is this love affair of yours? It is time you took a wife. You will be a king's son soon — God save King David.' "

The speaker mimicked Regent Robert Stewart's voice. He stood up, waved his pewter pot towards an empty chair and addressed the other man:

"The King and Queen were not there, you know, but Regent Robbie bowed in mock politeness to their empty seats.

"'I mean no harm to him,' he said, 'But drink will be the death of him, and soon by his looks. This girl de Athyn now, a good pedigree, I grant you, but she'll bring you nae tocher, Alexander. And there is Phemie sitting by you, puir quine, with no man, and a rare parcel of land going with her!'

"That plump young woman, Euphemia of Ross, looked down at her hands and blushed.

"Alexander spoke with his mouth full of pie:

"'How can I marry when I've nae place to bide in? Gie me a castle

19

and I'll find the woman to go wi' it.' Robert Stewart laughed. 'A deal, my lad. I'll gie you Lochindorb.'

"Alexander looked at his father. 'I think you mean that. I'll have it. But only if you gie me the siller tae furbish it.'

"'And Phemie there?' asked his father.

"'I could do better— she could do worse.'"

John of the Isles stopped. He pushed the flask of malmsey over to his companion. Malcolm de Athyn struck his thigh, hard, and laughed.

"S'Blood! Lord John, you take off that family well! I can see the Bastard snarling at his father through a mouthful of meat! In honesty, is that how it happened?"

"That is how it happened, slick, quick and clarted wi perfidy, just like every deal made by Alexander Stewart. Och aye," continued John of the Isles, "He got Lochindorb and 500 merks from his father who was glad to be rid of that dour dark place in its watery wastes. By the end of '70 he was in, and his lady love wi' him. And Phemie, Countess of Ross? She'll learn some day never to take a Stewart for granted. She waited and planned and prepared. Then bang! came the news that her bold suitor had ridden his men north to Lochindorb and Mariota with him. Robert his father? Och, he raged and fumed and apologised for his son's misdemeanours to the Ross crowd. But he was too feart that his carnal secret would ever get out to do more than rant at Alexander. He was mighty glad to win clear of the wench without a showdown with his wife. Forby, King David was dying and Robert wanted nae sharn to stick to his claes gin he mounted the throne."

"What of Alexander?" the other asked.

"Ach, possession is the law in Scotland and, short of an armed foray to the depths of Badenoch and starvation for his father's troops in these dreich forests and bogs, Alexander kens he is as safe up there as his father is here in Edinburgh — more so."

John MacDonald, Lord of all the Hebrides, looked at the young man across the table.

"It is my turn to ask the questions," he said. "Malcolm de Athyn, you and your family have better cause than most to hate King Robert and his Bastard. What does your sister Mariota think of the arrangement? Is she content to be Alexander Stewart's mistress, or does she hope to marry him?"

"Ye're real old fashioned, MacDonald, with your romantic island ideas of marriage and chivalry. I ken you're his brother-in-law, but don't ye know it would take a smart woman to break and harness that wild chiel. Mariota, by all accounts, has her own way of getting what she wants — from any man. I am her brother and I canna see how the wee wench does it. But at the age of nine she got this same young barbarian, after he had slockened our castle wi' Athyn's blood, to take her to safety, and those of our ill-used family who still lived. When I came back from Edinburgh with a troop from King David, God rest his soul, I was ower late to save my father, but the fiends who burned him were persuaded by Mariota to convoy our women in safety to the hospice of Portmoak. Young though she was, she stood up to Alexander Stewart as only a brave man would face a bear, and tamed him!"

John, Lord of the Isles, smiled to himself. The ways of these Scotsmen, and women, were not his ways, but there and then he made up his mind to visit Badenoch. Alexander he knew. He had been one of his wife Margaret's numerous brothers at their wedding and he had met him a year ago at the Coronation. But he had not seen this Mariota, that nighran, that poule! He would have to persuade Margaret. She would shy like a mare before a cat at the prospect of being the guest of Mariota de Athyn, but she liked her brother Alexander and was incurably inquisitive about other people's homes. If I put it to her carefully, he thought, she might relish the opportunity of comparing Alexander's new place at Lochindorb with her own castle at Ardtornish.

"Malcolm de Athyn," he said, "I wish your sister well, but I cannot see Robert Stewart, now that he is King, allowing that relationship

21

much peace, especially with the lands of Ross still on offer. It is no secret that my business at Court is to persuade my father-in-law, the King, to pursue this matter of a match between his family and Eufame. Were my own sons older I would spur them to that goal myself. If the Islands and Ross were united, with our two families bonded in double marriage, there would be good cause to hope that my subjects and the King's subjects would ally themselves against the English. Then, with the might of France behind us and the threat of war in Ireland, we would show the Plantagenets their proper place. I'll tell ye this, de Athyn, for I perceive in you both intelligence and patriotism, if Robert Stewart cannot see the force of my argument, then Scotland deserves a better King. The Douglas and the Baliol émigrés will shed no tears for him — nor, I believe, will you!"

Five

A boisterous wind brushed away clouds that hung like locks of hair over the sun's face, and colour flashed from water and wood. The loch mirrored the sky and the green forest was fragmented into shapes and shades of juniper, birch, alder and willow. Shadows floated across the moor in the wake of the clouds, moss gleamed, emerald in the sunshine, and heather, purple as the bellying sail that pulled the women, the men and the horses across Lochindorb. The boat, flat-bottomed to allow its passengers to land dry-shod, was manned by four oarsmen and a broad-shouldered fellow at the helm. The ladies in their high pointed hats, laughed when the breeze tugged at their veils and at their skirts; the lords joked to each other; grooms strained to calm their nervous animals. It was a rich and colourful company, horses with polished harness and gleaming brass, squires in the liveries of their masters and the latter, peacock-like, in leather jerkins and breeches, ornamented scabbards and plumed hats. Chattering like starlings and gayest of all were the ladies, dressed in silken gowns of pinks and turquoise and brocaded cloaks to tame the wind.

Half a mile ahead swam the towers and battlemented walls of a castle that rose sheer from the water and, above it, the silver and blue standard of the Earl of Buchan and Lord of Badenoch. As the barge drew near, oars were backed and the clumsy craft creaked towards the watergate. They could now see men running inside the castle and hear the calls and commands of the captain of the guard.

John, Lord of the Isles, laughed at the disorder. He stooped a little and whispered to his wife.

"If your brother is out to impress, he is leaving it a little late. "

Men were being bullied into line in the narrow space beyond the curtain wall, by a shouting sergeant at arms.

"Smarten up you hen-brained villains. Stand firm and look less like a rabble and more like a Prince's guard."

Margaret gave her husband a hard look. "Could your wild crew at Ardtornish do any better?" she asked.

John grinned.

She was always quick to defend her brother, although he did not care overmuch for him. Alexander Stewart had grown up a sulky, prickly youth with a permanent scowl on his face and a hand on his sword-hilt. He was "the enfant terrible" of his family, insolent towards his brothers with whom he constantly fought and squabbled. He was only barely polite to his father whom he regarded as weak and stupid because he had sired half his family, including Alexander, as bastards before legitimising them by marrying their mother – and that only because of her constant nagging. Alexander had no time for wife-ridden men.

Margaret knew this. She had been brought up in a family of boys and there were not many things about them she had not discovered. She had fought male dominance since she was a baby and she knew that the battle would continue to her death-bed. It was a man's world and a woman could so quickly become one of their chattels. She was deeply religious. Having endured the stain of illegitimacy, the sacrament of marriage was the corner-stone of her life, once taken, never to be rejected, a contract with God which alone made sinful lust permissible. She had preserved her chastity for her husband and firmly intended to remain a virtuous if not always an obedient wife. When her brother Alexander jilted Eufame of Ross and stormed off to his mountain fortress with that creature Mariota de Athyn, she had been filled with rage and shame. He had defied his father and he now defied God.

As the Castle of Lochindorb drew nearer and larger, her simmering annoyance that she, Margaret, wife of John, Lord of the Isles, had allowed herself to be wheedled into this ghastly trip, came to the boil. She had nothing in common with this de Athyn woman and had no wish to accept her hospitality. When John persuaded her in Edinburgh to visit her brother and to see his new home on which he had spent a small fortune, she had scarcely considered Mariota. But now, as they were about to set foot within the castle of Lochindorb, it was of Mariota de Athyn and not her brother Alexander that she thought. The sly cat who had been bounced from bed to royal bed had now to be greeted by her as mistress of Lochindorb Castle, her hostess for as many days and nights as she could endure her company. From the superiority of her twenty-nine years she prepared herself to meet this coquette who, at the age of sixteen, had set all Scotland agog by snatching the King's unruly son from the wealthy Eufame of Ross. She would be polite, if she could, but she would not put herself out for that one!

Six

It was in the mid afternoon of the third day that Margaret found herself alone with Mariota. Alexander and John had ridden south to the river Spey to join the gillies in the netting of a big run of salmon. Mariota and Margaret rode with them to the summit of the pass and watched their men until they were like toy figures in the distance. The blue crests of the Cairngorms heaved themselves above their dark pine-clad valleys. The horsemen picked their way through clumps of juniper by the McDonnell croft at Auchtertipper and vanished into birch-woods that shimmered in a heat-haze of late summer.

"Let us look in on Mathew's wife," said Mariota. "She is near her time and this is her first."

The croft at Auchtertipper sat comfortably on its grassy knoll at the entrance to a shallow fold in the mountain. The burn that splashed from the hill gouged a small valley for itself and filled it with peaty earth. Mathew McDonnell's few rigs of oats were yellowing towards harvest; wood-smoke oozed through the thatched roof, and a rowan-bush, round and red, grew at the door to ward off the bad fairies.

A thin bent man with a rusty head and a long face came to the door and greeted Mariota with grave courtesy. "How is Jean?" she asked. "We have brought her some baked meats and some wine."

"She is as well — or as unwell — as can be expected," replied Mathew.

"Oh! you were always a gloomy fellow," said Mariota and led the way through the low door into a dark room half filled with smoke. Two small windows gave a glimmer of light, but they were no more than holes in the wall, barred to keep out vermin from the moor. When her companion hesitated, Mariota said, "Don't be so stuck-up, Margaret! Duck low and you will breathe easier."

Under the pall of smoke in a box-bed on the floor, they saw the pale face of Jean McDonnell and the humped swelling of her nine-month pregnancy. Her belly was the biggest part of her. All else has shrunk, thought Mariota. Fair freckly cheeks had wasted away. Eyes, dark-rimmed and large in the mirk, gazed fearfully from a pinched face.

"Your ladyship is over kind," she said. Her voice was toneless, her mouth dry and cracked.

"I have some wine to put colour in your cheeks and some tasty pieces from the Earl's table," Mariota began, then stopped as Jean's face creased into a grimace of pain When the spasm had passed, she asked, "Who will help you when your time comes?"

"Mathew will fetch the midwife from the Bridge of Carr," replied Jean McDonnell in a voice that was weak with fatigue.

Bent double, the two women left the house, their eyes streaming with the peat-reek. "Mathew," commanded Mariota. "You must hasten for the midwife now. Tell her that I send for her and that I will pay her." Mathew nodded his head. "And if she is in any doubt what to do – or you are in any doubt — take a message to me at the castle." They mounted and rode away.

"God help that poor woman and grant her an easy delivery," said Mariota. "Now, Lady Margaret, come. See who can ride first to the top of the Craig over there!" Crying encouragement to their horses, the two young women galloped across the moor on a bridle-path which wound to the summit of the highest of the hills that ringed Lochindorb.

They looked across miles of purple moor undulating to the distant forest of Darnaway.

"Mon dieu," exclaimed Mariota. "Is it not beautiful!" She turned to her companion, her oval face flushed, under hair like autumn wheat. "Well, Lady Margaret, what do you think of my new home?" she asked.

Margaret looked at her.

"Your castle?" she said softly. Mariota's lips closed. The bright face faded, just a little.

27

"Yes, Margaret, my castle, for as long as I can hold it."

"And that means for as long as you can hold the Earl of Buchan."

The frail fabric of their new companionship tore, as both had known it would and one had intended it should. Without looking away, Mariota allowed silence to gather between them and asked, "How young were you when you fell in love with John of the Isles?"

"Why, sixteen," Margaret replied.

"Did you then at sixteen consider that marriage to him was as important as being in love with him?" Mariota paused to allow her words to grow. "I know you came here intending to despise me. I saw it in the first look you gave me. 'That sinful woman!' you were thinking. But if marriage has not even been whispered by my Lord of Buchan, what can I do? I love him. I have always loved him even though he and his men burned my father and raped my sisters. I think he loves me, but it matters to him that I am not his father's choice though he pretends it doesn't. I hope we shall marry. For the present, I am utterly content to live as we are living. I am carrying his child and that, I believe, has joined us to each other more closely than even a marriage ceremony could have done. I ask you again what do you think of my house?"

Lady Margaret looked in astonishment at her companion, a new admiration tugging at her heart. She gazed down at Lochindorb. "I think you have done wonderfully. I can usually compare my own home at Ardtornish with others and feel no envy, but your island castle" – she emphasised the 'your' – "is most comfortable. Rising from those black depths it belies its stark exterior. From the moment I entered, I felt curiously at home. To begin with, I resented this as I resented you. You have managed, Mariota, to create cosiness and quaintness out of long twisting passages and cell-like tower rooms, which must have seemed a daunting prospect when you first saw them." Mariota's face glowed with pleasure. "I could not have made the changes I wanted to make, and which you have charmingly described, without Alexander's hard bargaining. He persuaded his father to part with a small ransom and he chose the craftsmen. You mention the tower rooms. Did you notice the views from the four out-facing windows?"

"I have only been in one – the one nearest us, the one with Lord Jesus crucified." Margaret hesitated. "Where did you get such a beautiful thing? It made me blush and made me wonder too at its barbarity. Whoever carved it left nothing to imagine. There is a manliness about him that makes that moment before he died both tragic and horrifying!"

Mariota rested a hand on Margaret's arm. "You have seen the Christ-man, just as I have seen him and I worship him the more because of the sacrifice of his body. O Margaret! Is it awful to think of Jesus as a man? Is it sinful to imagine that God had excelled in endowing him with the physical perfections of other men? I have often covered my head in shame that I should think so, but was he not as mortal as we and was he not different from us only because he conquered the desires and lusts that tempt all of us, me – and you too? For a woman to admire his shapeliness cannot be too great a sin?"

Margaret looked at her intense and anxious face and said, "Women are expected to be more Christlike than men. How unfair life has been to you, Mariota de Athyn. You have been befriended by the very man who planned and executed your father's death and you believe you love him. God has endowed you with so much beauty and frailty. Why then should you not seek out the beauty and the frailty in our Saviour?" She paused. "Do not plunge too deeply in such a sea, or you may drown. If we excuse ourselves of our sins because of Him, we miss the blessing of confessing those sins before Him and of his forgiveness.

"O Margaret, how wise you are!" cried Mariota. "I think I shall always remember our conversation on this mountain-top, when I showed you how the Devil tempts me and you rebuffed him." She sighed. "Alas, alone, I cannot often expel the Devil from my soul. And sometimes I do not even try! Purgatory was designed for such as me!"

Seven

Lady Margaret MacDonald was never to forget the twenty-four hours that followed her conversation with Mariota de Athyn on the summit of Craig Tiribeg. Before dawn – she had been in her bed it seemed only a short time – Mariota came to her room. "I must go to Mathew's croft. He has sent for me. Will you come too?" They had talked of this possibility. It was certainly not an undertaking she would have given at home to any of John's crofters, who, anyway, always seemed besieged by helpers in times of travail. But she had been shocked at the loneliness of this poor girl about to bear her first baby in her cot far out in the moors with only her doleful husband as company and she was amazed at Mariota's solicitude. So when she had rubbed the sleep from her eyes she sprang from her bed and said simply, "What shall I wear?" Mariota was dressed in a pair of the Earl's old breeches and had pulled a knitted garment over her head. With her knee-boots she looked like a boy. "Here you are," she replied and laid a collection of clothes across the bed. "We must hurry, but with luck we shall be back before the servants are properly roused. Don't worry if you look like a tinker."

A lantern moon hung high in the sky and the path to Auchtertipper was black against the dusky haze of heather.

"Have you done this often?" asked Margaret.

"When I was little I watched the herdsmen and the shepherds pull the young from their dam's womb. I have helped, too, at the birth of my friends' babies," said Mariota, "and they were not all easy. I hope I am wrong, but I think Jean McDonnell is going to have a hard time. She is too thin, with little bust and no hips. Big, hippy women are the best breeders – like yourself!"

Mariota was not wrong. They heard the shrieks of the labouring woman even before they caught sight of the taper in the window of the croft. The midwife from the Bridge of Carr had brought her three bairns with her and her husband – Lady Lochindorb was paying – and the children crouched in a corner, terrified. The midwife herself was large and coarse and smelled like rancid butter. Sweat gleamed in her hair and dripped from her dirty fingers on to the belly on the bed – a belly which rocked and groaned and strained, a belly that was all they could see of poor Jean, it and two sticks of arms that threshed and clung and gripped and fought.

"Stand back, woman, and let me see what is happening," commanded Mariota.

"Naething's happening," panted the midwife, struggling to free herself from the despairing clutch.

"Jean," shouted Mariota. "Jean, stop fighting us. I am here to help you."

For a moment the struggling and the screaming stopped. Mariota swiftly parted the knees and looked between them. "God," she whispered. "A breech!" She knelt between the woman's legs and slipped her hands up the sides of the baby's hips.

"Hold her legs apart," she commanded as Jean twisted and strained. The midwife's husband held Jean's hands and tried to prise them out of Mathew's hair. Mariota reached inside and with a finger pulled down a tiny foot, then another, and the breech stuck out obscenely between its mother's thighs.

"Get her backside up," shouted Mariota. "Mathew, put a pair of stout poles across the bed and support Jean's bum between the two. Jean, Jean, it's almost over now. Let me help you a little more." The legs and back and arms of the baby hung like a rag-doll from its mother's womb, twitched, then the whole baby dropped into Mariota's hands. She let out a cry of triumph. "It's a maid, Jean lass, and it lives!"

She held the limp little body by its ankles and smacked the blue bottom. Then again. The baby heaved and coughed and, oh! blessed sound, cried and cried and cried.

The midwife grabbed the wee mite from Mariota and said

brusquely, "I can manage fine. I'll hae the caul and the afters awa in nae time." Mariota looked at Mathew's long ashen face.

"Mathew," she said, "Fetch me a bucket of clean water."

To Jean, when at last the afterbirth came free in a gush of blood, she said, "I'll send you a wet-nurse and all the blankets you need tomorrow. Those skinny paps have no milk in them."

Eight

Margaret was still in bed when her husband and her brother returned at noon. They were in bad fettle, cross, tired and filthy. Alexander stood at the loch-side and roared towards his castle: "Boatman! Come quickly or I'll have your balls for breakfast!"

They had caught no fish, they had cursed the ghillies and they had ridden hard for home. The ghillies' tale that there had been a huge run of fish in the pools yesterday did not help the Earl of Buchan's temper, for the Spey had risen a foot with a thunderstorm in the Monadhliath mountains and the run of salmon had swept on.

By the time they sat down at supper, Alexander's temper had been smoothed. In the dusk of her bedroom Mariota had recounted the excitements of her early morning and, in the telling, subtly distracted her man from his angry thoughts. When they met John and Margaret at table, Alexander's black mood had gone, miraculously replaced, thought Margaret, by boisterous good humour.

"The King," said John of the Isles, "has asked me to journey to Acre in the Holy Land next year to ransom our friends who were captured in the ill-fated attack of '69. He suggested that you, my lord, would add distinction to my company." John of the Isles smiled and continued. "As we shall be away for some time it occurred to me that it will be unwise to expose these ladies to the temptations of loneliness."

All within earshot paused, each with his own thoughts. It was well known that a ransom demand had been delivered for six Scottish knights captured by the Saracens on a raid on Antioch and it was rumoured that the figure expected for their release was greater than the treasury could afford, even after extortionate levies on the relatives and on the possessions of the victims.

Alexander, who had no illusions about his father's generosity, thought, "Poor bastard. He knows he will lose face with the rest of Christendom if he lets these fellows rot in a Saracen dungeon, yet he must have been squeezed flat by the Estates before he agreed to such a sum of gold being paid."

Margaret looked at her handsome John and thought, "How wise of the King to choose him as emissary."

But to Mariota other horizons had appeared. A journey to the world's end! Perilous, but oh! the adventure of it! The chance to see peoples she had heard the troubadours sing about, to visit strange outlandish places with magical names and to feel all about her the scents and tastes and sounds of the colourful East. In a dream she heard Alexander say, "If the Estates have approved the ransom, there will be a safe-conduct to secure from King Edward. Do you think the English will agree to such a treasure being taken through their land when ransom for our late and unlamented King David is still unpaid?"

"You miss the point, Alexander," John said. "Why do you think your father chose me to lead the expedition? My fleet makes safe-conduct through England irrelevant. My vessels will carry us and the gold to France where we can be assured of an unmolested journey to the Mediterranean."

"And Edward, if he finds out, can do nothing. Even his English pirates will not dare match themselves against the warships of John of the Isles!" Margaret said proudly.

Mariota looked at Alexander, her eyes bright and big, her mouth pursed by the question she dared not ask. She thought, "Is this the moment? Do I know he will agree? I could not bear it if he refused me." She glanced at Margaret, since last night her friend, then turned boldly towards Stewart.

"On such a long journey there would be many things that women like Margaret and me can do for you. But perhaps your Royal father will not agree." Despite herself her voice trembled. Would Alexander laugh at her in his hateful, cruel way, or would he laugh and agree with her? She added, as if it explained her nervousness, "My baby will be born in three months and will be weaned next year."

"What in heaven's name has that got to do with it? Child or no child, you will come with me and the King can look down his long nose and be damned!" She laughed with him. She had done it! She would see those wonderful fairy-tale places! She touched his hand. Roughly, but not too roughly, he pushed her away. "What do you say then, Margaret? Will you risk your husband's poor seamanship in his leaky craft to accompany us? You will? Brave girl. Then, John, you will be chief navigator. I will be your body-guard and these two bright charmers our boatswain and coxswain!" He laughed at his joke. "Navigate us then John of the Isles, to the lands of love, lechery and daring – do!" John raised his flagon to the company, "Near to the land of Jesus and yet safe from the Saracen's sword, we shall find our haven. While you, Alexander, and I visit the Emir of Acre and bargain with him under the flag of truce, those ladies must rest in safety. My friend, you allude to the lands of love, lechery and daring – do. There is such a haven where love is paramount – the realm of Aphrodite, the island of Cyprus! Island of blue sky and warm sea, orange-blossom at springtime, mimosa in the summer. When I was a boy I followed my father on such an expedition. We sailed in search of the fabulous island that the Viking Magnus of Man discovered many hundreds of years ago – an island of copper and gold! And we found it! We did not slay and rob as Magnus did. We bartered and returned laden with copper. Richard Coeur de Lion on his way to his Crusade conquered it and all because his beloved princess had been unmannerly treated. I shall make a glorious return to the island of shepherds and nymphs and we shall sport on the very strand which, Homer tells us, received the gentle feet of Aphrodite, Goddess of Love. We shall deliver our friends from the fortress of the Saracen and make an Odyssey that all Scots shall remember!"

Alexander Stewart scowled his acknowledgement and his envy of his friend's rhetoric but Mariota clapped her hands in sheer delight and exclaimed, "I cannot wait to be there!"

Nine

Three vessels of war sailed in the spring of '72 from Castle Tioram in Loch Moidart on the western coast of Scotland. They were commanded by John of the Isles, Alexander Irvine of Drum and Alexander Stewart of Badenoch. Each was defended by armed men and provisioned to carry the ladies and such other attendants as befitted the importance of the venture. They took with them in three chests 5000 gold merks, separately carried on the three ships to diminish the possibility of total loss. Before leaving the Scottish seas Mariota persuaded the captains to drop anchor in the Solway Firth.

"I have dreamed," she told Margaret, "of Lady Devorgilla Baliol, that saintly woman, who came to me dressed in silks and silver and bearing an ivory casket to her bosom. As she approached, she opened the casket and said to me 'This is my true love, my sweet, silent, companion,' and in my dream I saw the blood-red heart of her husband. 'Mariota,' she said, 'Pray for me and for all good women.'"

Margaret was amazed. "Lady Devorgilla has been dead for eighty years. Her ghost must surely be at rest by now!" "She visited me in a dream and therefore cannot be at peace," said Mariota. "I only know I must not continue on this perilous journey until I do as she has asked. I shall kneel at her tomb and pray for her soul, or disaster will strike us all."

Her persistence and her conviction overcame the exasperation of the men and so the small fleet, only two days sail from home, turned up the Solway on the tide and anchored at the mouth of the Nith. Dressed in white, Margaret, Philomena Irvine and Mariota were ferried across the wind-chopped estuary. They walked through small meadows of new clover, passing hedgerows, white in May blossom, to the ruins of the Abbey of Dulce Corde. Nettles stung when they clambered over fallen masonry to the high altar and the tomb of Devorgilla. With their finger-nails, they scraped away moss from stone and exposed the elegy and haltingly Mariota read aloud the Latin inscription. "Grant o King most high, the attainment of rest to Devorgilla, whom, with the heart of her husband, likewise this stone covereth." The three knelt on damp grey slabs and wept for the soul of the pious woman whose love inspired monks of old to call that ruined place "Sweetheart Abbey". On her grave they laid posies of white flowers on blackthorn stems. "Requiescas in pace, Devorgilla," said Mariota.

Ten

The three ships that sailed from Moidart in the spring of 1372 disembarked their passengers in the estuary of the Loire. From thence the knights, their ladies and their attendants rode slowly south. Philomena Irvine had nearly died of sickness at sea and they rested a while in Nantes to speed her recovery. Then illness ravaged the party in the hill country of Tarn. Stewart swore they had all been poisoned and was so racked by pain and fever that those who were able kept a watch on him lest he murder the inn-keeper. By now it was high summer. For weeks they had been in the saddle and the smell of their own bodies made them sick. Only when the bright shimmer of the ocean appeared in the distance did their spirits lighten. Thank God, they would spend no more nights in squalid inns, scratching, on flea-infested straw. In Marseilles they would at last find comfortable lodging.

While they rode south, the ships and their crews beat against the westerlies along the coast of Iberia, then ran with the wind to Africa and the Pillars of Hercules. It was a long cruel journey which only seamen could have survived and the exhausted crews rejoiced when they put into port in the south of France. Free, until their masters arrived, they had time to repair their battered ships and time also to enjoy the debauchery with which all sailormen were supplied by the touts and the prostitutes of Marseilles.

In that colourful and noisy port something happened which seemed unimportant at the time, but for which Mariota was to be profoundly grateful. She was riding with Alexander to the harbour. One of the ship's masters had reported difficulties in obtaining a new tiller and Alexander was anxious to sail. He hated these French towns – he hated towns anywhere – and he suspected the delay was chiefly due to the procrastination of a pleasure-loving sailor spinning out his shore-time.

The street ahead was jammed with people. There was a slave auction. Captives were being sold to galley owners and from horseback they could see the ring. A movement in the crowd around the auctioneer caught their attention. A small dark man with his hands tied put down his head like a bull and charged at the buyers. He was tethered by a long piece of rope to a big negro and the crowd roared at his antics. Mariota watched him. He was quite the ugliest little man she had ever seen. His legs were short and his body long. His head was large in comparison with the rest of him. He had black bushy eyebrows and no ears. His nose was flattened on his face and, while he was mock-fighting the crowd, he sang an English sea-shanty in a fine tenor voice. The auction-master made little progress. The bidding had stopped at six francs – no one wanted such a small man.

On an impulse Mariota called out, "Trente francs pour le petit." There was a hush and all heads turned to see who had put up the bid. There was a shout of laughter from the mob as the little fellow blew a kiss towards his new purchaser. Alexander was angry.

"What do you want with that object?" he demanded.

"I don't know yet," Mariota smiled back at him, "But I am sure I will find a use for him."

The dwarf was at her side, dancing and capering to the laughing crowd, and she dipped into her purse and handed him thirty silver coins.

"Take this to the auction-master and come back, free, to me."

"Free, madam? Free?" The little man's mouth fell open. "You said free?"

"I said free," replied Mariota.

The prisoner took the coins and pulled himself up the rope as if climbing a rigging. Then, when his wrists were untied, he somersaulted and hand-sprung all the way back to his new mistress with the crowd roaring applause. "You have a bargain, madam," he said. "For thirty pieces, the sum that Judas sold Our Lord, you have bought a dwarf, a clown, an acrobat with a most powerful and pleasing voice." He stopped, snatched off his woollen skull cap to reveal his shining bald head, bowed and looked up at Mariota.

"You are right, madam." His voice was low and soft and he spoke only for her.

"Why should you pay for a man-slave when you can enslave all men!"

He grasped her horse's bridle and drew her safely through the crowd, the rabble withdrawing before them like waves on a shore.

Mariota never regretted her purchase. He told her he was called "The Hawk", because he was all eyes and no ears and was as bald as a vulture, and within a short time he had become a favourite with all the Scots. "You have made me your freedman my lady," he said to her in front of Alexander, "But I will always remain your chattel to use as it pleases you."

A wind that blew south toward Africa sped the three vessels on their long voyage to Cyprus. Their safety depended on careful navigation and on remaining close enough to each other to give the small fleet protection from the creeping assault of pirates. The sea around Sardinia was infested by these but single or disabled ships were the prey they sought. At Cagliari they took water aboard and at St Paul's Bay in Malta they revictualled.

"I suppose, Mariota, you will wish to kneel on those ragged rocks where Saul was shipwrecked and pray for the souls of all good mariners?" Alexander taunted her with her piety. He was surprised by her reply. "I would not kneel for that old woman-hater were it to save the last man alive in Christendom!"

Blown by the wind from Greece towards Alexandria and then north by the hot dry breath of the levant, they made landfall off Cyprus near the ancient city of Paphos. Four months after they had watched the snow-capped peaks of Mull slip behind them into the ocean, after a hundred days on horseback and at sea, they dropped anchors in the clear green waters of Famagusta Bay. In a gondola, John of the Isles was ferried ashore to affirm the peaceful aspirations of his fighting ships and to present letters of greeting from Robert, King of the Scots, to King Peter of Cyprus. He returned with the news that the King had been murdered and that the Court was plunged into mourning that would continue until the young Prince. was crowned.

The spirits of the voyagers were not dampened.

"At last," sighed Mariota, "At last to rest in soft beds, bathe in clean water and live the languid life of a royal courtier on this sun-blessed island."

Their slow progress through France had introduced the Scots to a life so different from their own that those, like Mariota, who had never journeyed from her own wild country found amazement at every mile and marvelled at the wealth they saw in every town they entered.

But all had been a mere shadow compared to the spendour of Famagusta. The bustle of the harbour, where gilded, painted ships from all the world nodded to each other on the gentle swell and where the Scottish warships looked like paupers at a wedding, had still not prepared them for the magnificence of the town. Fortified by bastions fifty feet high and twenty feet thick, the city impressed its impregnability and its importance on all who entered. Within these mighty walls churches, Gothic and Byzantine, squatted by markets and fountained squares where rich merchants and cheap vendors, black, brown, olive and white, sold everything from pearls to pomegranates, from milking goats to pretty youths with painted faces. As their men forced their horses through the throng, the ladies explored with their eyes, their ears and especially with their noses the abundant life; the animals, the grey, white and pink pigeons that soared in wheeling flocks, and especially the people, all shapes and sizes, laughing, weeping, cajoling, whispering.

Everywhere there was colour. Wistaria, clematis and Bougainvillaea cascaded from the walls. Splashes of pink and red geranium glowed

41

from hidden gardens, from porches, and from balconies shaded by vines, heavy with grapes. Mariota thought how beautiful and incongruous these would look draped in such profusion on the grey battlements of Lochindorb! The city overflowed with gold, for, in the years since the Saracens had captured Acre, merchants had descended upon this Cypriot port and made it the wealthiest in the world. These merchants were richer, 'twas said, than the Kings of Christendom.

The Scottish party was lodged in a house adjacent both to the palace and to the towering buttresses of the Cathedral of St Nicholas and were promised audience of Queen Eleanor and Prince Peter on the seventh day following their arrival. The ladies insisted on new clothes for their consorts and fresh dresses for themselves. When the men objected to the expense, Mariota said in exasperation that if they wished to meet the Queen of the richest island in the world clothed like Hebridean pirates that was their affair. She would prefer to represent Scotland in a different light and had chosen glowing brocades and silks of Cathay.

The Court of the royal family of Cyprus should have reflected the gaiety and flamboyance of their subjects. And so, thought Mariota, it may well have done – but not now. The shadow of King Peter's violent death hung like a pall of smoke over the palace and the vivacious Genoese and Venetians, Armenians and Greeks who formed the upper crust of Cypriot society were about as happy and as friendly as a pack of whipped hounds.

The description was Alexander Irvine's. During the long journey, Irvine, lord of Drum, had become the darling of the ladies and a favourite with the men. He was as solidly dependable as his castle in Mar and as square in his dealings with others. He seldom spoke but to lift the mood of the company and, although unskilled in the foppery of etiquette, his judgement was accurate and his chivalry un-questioned. In choosing him to join his team of negotiators, John of the Isles had decided wisely, for in the protracted bargaining ahead Irvine of Drum proved he could match the cunning of the Saracen Wizier.

"I have not had reason to whip a whole pack of hounds, but no doubt, if I had, I would have preferred their company to these people," commented Stewart. "The Court is riddled with gossip and suspicion. They hint that the boy's uncle is his father's murderer." The Scots rode together towards the harbour down a track that wound its way across the sands of golden bays lapped by blue-green translucent water, between dusty carob-trees and through groves of figs and olives. There seemed no reason for caution or for protection in this peaceful place. They had been warned of brigands who lived in the deep valleys and wooded slopes of Mount Olympus but here by the shore, five miles from Famagusta, the only brigands were small clouds of flies and needle-sharp mosquitos. But it had become a way of life of the Scot to move in groups, and armed, such was the lawless state of his own poor land.

Mariota listened to Stewart's opinion of the royal murder and exclaimed, "How unnatural it would be for the dead King's brother to be also his murderer! All can see that John of Antioch, as he is called, is besotted with love for the boy's mother and she, the Queen, seems intent on encouraging him. Were he her husband's murderer would she be so passive and forgiving?"

"Mariota, you may be worldly-wise in some things but you can be a simple child in others." Alexander Stewart chuckled. "If you grew tired of me would you not encourage a lover to murder me?" They reached the top of a small hill overlooking the bay and the harbour. In the three weeks since they had arrived in Famagusta their ships had been prepared again for sea. Now, black tarred hulls shone with white upperworks; masts were crimson; faded brown canvas had been replaced by sails of royal purple and embroidered on each was the coat of arms of Scotland. The rigging was black rope and the painted castles at bow and poop gleamed in gold.

"How beautiful they look!" exclaimed Margaret. "Fit now for the King of the Isles?" laughed her husband. "And a Prince of the Realm," added Stewart. Irvine smiled and remarked, "Bastard though he may be!" They all laughed. It was that sort of day, full of brightness and gaiety, and these fair ships seemed to secure the success of the mission. Philomena made her little speech. "Brave captains," she said, "return to us soon and in safety and we shall welcome you with open arms." Mariota touched her lover, looked solemnly up into his dark eyes and added, "and with open legs, my bonny man."

On the following day the three galleys, oared from the harbour, heeled in the wind and headed east. High on the battlements the ladies and their attendants watched them sail away. Soon the vessels became toy ships, bright sails filled and white water bubbling in their wake. Within an hour they had gone, melted, it seemed, into the dazzling blue of the ocean.

Eleven

John of the Isles sat at table with his head in his hands and his big shoulders shook as he wept.

"In the name of Jesus," asked Stewart, "what has become of our leader? What is it, man, that has turned you into a blubbering woman?" MacDonald thrust a letter at him. "Read it. Read it aloud," he said. "Perhaps I have dreamt it. Perhaps I have imagined all that is written there."

Stewart passed the missive to Irvine. "You can read. Tell us quickly what has sucked the manhood from our friend."

Irvine took the letter while the others watched and waited. He stood with his back to sunlight that poured in from an azure sky and from the white walls and warehouses of the harbour. Beyond rose the forest of Saracen towers and minarets surrounding the dome of the Christian church of Peter and Paul, a scene that reminded the Scots sharply of their own insecurity in this alien land. They heard the strange high song of the muezzins in their towers calling the faithful to prayer.

"This was written a week ago," began Irvine, "and Margaret, John's wife, has put her seal to it. 'My dear lord,' she says, 'make haste to return, for we are in a piteous and perilous state. We are besieged in the Castle of St Hilarion by a Genoese army and are in terror for our lives. You have been so long in coming that we fear you have forgotten us and much has happened since you set sail. In the spring, King Peter was crowned and we joined in celebration with the Court of Queen Eleanor and Prince John of Antioch. It was an occasion of happiness and thanksgiving. But as the King was nearing St Nicholas Cathedral a squabble broke out between the Venetian and the Genoese guards. My lord, that a matter of such small importance could place us in such jeopardy! The quarrel was of protocol and within minutes the great courtyard of the cathedral had become a battlefield. The young King's commands went unheeded and we fled the city. My lord, the bloodshed leaped from street to street as we have seen fire leap in the Forest of Lorn. We sought refuge in the Castle of St Hilarion near Kyrenia, for when we neared Nicosia the war had spread ahead of us even to the capital. Dearly beloved, we are now prisoners in this mountain fortress. Genoese troops from over the sea have invaded the island. All is blamed on the King and when we surrender, as in time we must, I fear you will see us no more. We hear of deeds beyond description which make us even envy the dead. Let me describe to you how twenty men died here in this fortress and of the manner of their going. I tell you about these horrors my lord only to spur you to our rescue.

"'Since we came to this island of Cyprus we have remarked on how much in love is Prince John of Antioch with Queen Eleanor and how coolly she has played on his emotions. In the Court it was rumoured, but in whispers, that he had arranged the murder of his brother the King so that he could wed her. It is plain now that she must have planned to be revenged on him. Oh! my husband, how wicked can be the thoughts behind a smiling face! To Hilarion, John retreated with his Bulgarian guards – giants of men as honest as they were stupid. The Queen professed to dislike them from the start. She called them verminous stinking oafs (with good reason). She maintained they were not to be trusted (which was not so) and gradually her "suspicions" ate into the heart of Prince John. One night, not long since, he summoned the guard singly to the battlements and caused each to be thrown to his death on the jagged rocks beneath. Then, when he was without his bodyguard, the Queen openly threatened to destroy him as he had destroyed his men. Fearing for his life he fled the castle. O God! His fate was worse than the fate of his faithful Bulgarians. He was taken by the Genoese before he was out of our sight, and in full view of the castle he was tied to a stake and flayed alive. We covered our ears to his screams as he begged for death.

46

"'My lord, we fear the barbarous Genoese, but we fear them rather less than we now fear Queen Eleanor. She is mad. She spends her days in solitary brooding and makes the nights hideous with her threats. All share her hatred, foes and friends alike.

"'Sweet Heart, for the sake of Mariota and Philomena and of your own beloved wife come quickly to lead us from this hellish place.'"

Irvine stopped and a tense silence enveloped the room.

They had been in Acre for nine months. Week by week the Saracen gently pawed them like a playful cat, wearing down their resolve, sometimes by lavish entertainment sometimes by weeks of silence and inactivity. When it seemed at last their offer would be accepted and that they could collect the captives and sail for home, the bargaining would start again and their hopes would evaporate. The enemy was determined to extract their last gold coin before parting with the prisoners. Although captives for so long, the six knights had been well treated, which, according to their captors, increased their value. "Were they tormented, broken, rags of men, they would be set free for a pittance, would they not. But, fed and cared for like kings, by Allah they are worth much more." So it had gone on and, when they were no nearer to success than when they had arrived, came this letter which demanded their return at once to Cyprus.

MacDonald's head was sunk on the table.

"Hopeless, hopeless," he muttered. "We can do nothing to help them. God forgive us, Margaret, you will all die."

Alexander Stewart stepped forward and gripped him roughly by the shoulders. "Rouse yourself, man. They must not die. Remember this, that the young King is with them and only he can command the garrison to surrender."

"Pray that he has courage," said Irvine. Stewart paused, then, addressing himself mainly to MacDonald, he said, "I have heard that the castle Hilarion is the strongest in the island, built by Richard Coeur de Lion and built well, I'll wager, for it was a safe love-nest for his lady Princess Berengaria of Navarre. I learn these things from

Mariota who also tells me that the castle was known of old as 'Dieu d'Amour' – though by sweet Jesus there will be no love between us and these accursed Genoese."

"How then can we with three score men defeat a whole army astride the approaches of a castle, however impregnable?" John of the Isles had at last regained some composure. "God in Heaven, what can we do?"

"We shall sail at once," shouted Stewart. "Be damned to logic. We must try. The lives of our women depend on it."

"But if we leave we also leave the captives we came so far to free," retorted MacDonald.

"Faint Heart!" Stewart banged a fist on the table. "We can achieve in one stroke what we have come to do and save our ladies as well, God be on our side. For we shall tell the Emir we go first to fight for our wives against the Genoese and that when we have conquered we shall resume our negotiations. My guess is that we shall so astonish the Saracen by our audacity that when we return he will settle at last for our ransom offer!"

His guess was very near the truth. When the Emir was told that the Scottish knights with their three score men were bound for Cyprus to take on the Genoese army he summoned them to his palace. "I make you this offer, most noble knights of Skottisland. My Sultan, Mohammet Sulliman the Invincible, admires your audacity and has commanded me to provide ships and provisions for two hundred of his Janizaries who will assist you in your gallant plan. All these fighting men – the flower of his army – he will send with you, freely, on condition that you fulfil my modest demands concerning the release of my prisoners.

The three men dared not so much as glance at each other, lest they showed their surprise and their delight. Here was a way to ransom the prisoners with no loss of face for either party, and a real chance for them to rescue their ladies. John of the Isles stepped forward and bowed to the Emir.

"Most gracious before lord Allah," he said, "you may tell the Invincible Mohammet Sulliman, Sultan of Arabia, that we accept these terms. We shall gladly lead his men and shed our blood with theirs. Tell the Invincible Mohammet that all booty shall be shared with his captains when we have slaughtered the Genoese and succoured our ladies. Tell him we bow to his wishes and to his wisdom."

Twelve

"And this," quoth John of the Isles as his ship glided from the harbour, "this, happily concludes the long drawn-out bargaining for the lives of our prisoners – happily, that is, should we be successful. The Sultan gets his gold, we get reinforcements and the captive knights their freedom. All now depends on God." He looked back at the fleet he commanded. The three Scottish galleons rode high and proud above the waves, their billowing square sails majestic; and in their wake the ships of Islam, low dhows with raked masts and curved triangular sail, twelve of them, packed tight with armed men. The Janizaries stood shoulder to shoulder, their blue-gray herons' plumes unmistakable above their white robes. And under those robes, John mused, hung the long wicked curved scimitars so feared by the crusaders.

The minarets and domes of Acre slipped over the sea's edge as a strong, steady wind blew the fleet swiftly towards Cyprus.

Alexander Stewart of Badenoch, no stranger to war, stood on his poop deck and counted the ships. "By what strange fate," he said, "are three Christian knights with their six newly freed comrades leading a Janizary force of two hundred warriors into battle against a Christian army? And such warriors! Ideal fighting men! The elite of the Ottoman troops! Soldiers reserved for the most desperate tasks, to stem a rout or to turn a wavering advance into total victory." They were all of that, these fighting men, who had been taken as children from Christian communities engulfed by the tide of Ottoman conquest. Disciplined to the point of death, the best became the elite of a Sultan's army. They were formidable foes, forbidden marriage so that their temper remained iron-hard, unsoftened by affection. They were well named, reflected Stewart, 'The merciless sword of Allah.'

The hated enemy! And now at his command. He thought then of the battle to come, the flash of steel in moonlight – the attack had to come after dark against the more numerous foe – the slashing, the cutting, the stabbing, the grunts of the smitten, blood to the elbows and arms heavy with killing. They planned to make landfall at Morphu Bay and march through the dusk into a night battle on the slopes of Hilarion.

Uplifted by the thought of war, their ships in the van of this fleet, the three Scottish knights in that moment of high exaltation all but forgot the reason for the slaughter, the blood-letting. Their ladies might not have existed!

The wind blew steadily and the fleet surged like angry swans towards Cyprus. They made their landing at dusk on a deserted beach and before the moon rose over the twin peaks of Didymus they fell on the unsuspecting Genoese. Caught at their cooking-fires which beaconed their position and their strength, they were slaughtered where they sat, hot oven-bread in their mouths and the smell everywhere of roasting kid. Taken by surprise and from behind, within minutes, it seemed, three hundred sweeping scimitars and swords had demolished an army. Those who ran were pursued and cut down. Those who surrendered were massacred. The conquerors wiped their reddened steel on the tents of the enemy then sat down to finish off the food in their cooking-pots and in their ovens. The pay-chest of the Genoese army, the silver and the gold of their dead captives, were divided among the victors. On captured horses the Scots rode to the castle of St Hilarion. The gates were thrown open and the knights were admitted and acclaimed by the garrison as only those who have lived near to death can acclaim their saviours. And later that day they were welcomed by their ladies as Philomena had described and as Mariota had promised!

The Janizaries returned to their ships. The Scots learned that they had proceeded slowly to the shore, devastating in three days all the lands between Hilarion and Morphu Bay, plundering three monasteries and looting six villages.

"The villains must have sailed for home well pleased with their booty," remarked John of the Isles when he heard of this.

"I'll wager they made time between prayers to enjoy the women they found," exclaimed Alexander Stewart. "They care and live only for three things, slaughter, rape and the love of Allah!"

Thirteen

Because the Genoese army in the west had been destroyed, the Scots were hailed as demigods and greatly feted. The war between the King and the invader was far from won, but news of the victory at Hilarion put heart into the King's supporters and his small but growing army now controlled the long fertile plain between the mountains and the sea. At Kyrenia, the castle had held out against the enemy, although the abbey had been torn apart and its monks in their white habits slaughtered. Some said it was the invaders from Genoa who desecrated that holy place, but others swore the destroyers were a chanting cohort of tall white-robed soldiers who appeared out of nowhere and vanished into thin air.

The Queen mother had regained her composure and her wits and pressed the Scots to remain as her bodyguard, but to the relief and joy of their womenfolk the three knights declined and set about preparing their ships for the long voyage home. Rich gifts of precious jewels were presented to Mariota, Margaret and Philomena. King Peter made substantial payment for the timeous relief of his castle and for his rescue, and in the months that followed the battle the knights were indulged as only heroes are, by everyone, including their wives. "We leave Cyprus with more gold than the Janizaries stole," John of the Isles remarked as he watched his ships take on food and wine for their journey.

"And no doubt we leave on the island fewer women to hide their shame!" added Stewart.

Mariota stood with him on the shore as barrels of wine, jars of sugar, boxes containing silks, leatherwork, combs, brocades, jewellery, and pots beautifully designed and coloured were rowed out to the galleons at anchor in the bay. She pouted her lips and looked up at him.

"Since we came to this island a year ago, we have only seen our men during a few weeks of that time and, although we have had no lack of admirers, we have been too miserable and frightened even to acknowledge their attentions. I shudder when I think of our ordeal. We shall not remember Cyprus as Aphrodite's Isle, that is certain, but more as the abode of Murder. I will not be sorry to return to the green hills and soft mists of Scotland. As for women who have to hide their shame, I am proud to be again with child! " She hugged her lover's arm.

"He will be called Walter I think – a name not in the Holy Book and therefore not in use in this priest-ridden island. There are occasions, my beloved, when memory becomes a pain and never will I cease to love this child I carry, because of a name."

The safe-conduct given to them by the Emir of Acre allowed their ships to be restocked at the Moorish ports of Cartagena and Algeciras before sailing between The Pillars of Hercules into the great ocean beyond. God or Allah smiled on them and sent a sailor's wind to carry them northwards.

Many moons after leaving Cyprus they dropped anchor again on the sands of Solway, and Mariota, Philomena and Margaret knelt once more over the bones of Devorgilla and gave thanks to her for bearing them safely through peril and rapine. It was now autumn and to the brittle nettles among the fallen stones were added sticky burrs and sharp thistles which dragged at their skirts and stabbed at their thighs. Brambles grew across the grave and Philomena cried out in pain as the spiky vines caught her ankles. Both she and Mariota were by now heavy with child – a fate, Margaret said, she had avoided in Cyprus only because she had used her wits as much as she had used her body!

The long journey ended for Mariota amid the ripening bracken of the Badenoch moors. The gales of the equinox had not yet arrived to strip the oaks and birches and the reflections of russet and gold on lonely tarns made her weep for joy. The ferryman rowed them out to the castle, silent and strong within its grey walls, which, on that still,

September day, were mirrored to the smallest detail on the surface of the loch. She looked at her bearded man and said, "I have wept for this moment ever since that frightening day when the war began in the cathedral square of Famagusta. I shall explode with joy, I think, when I hold my little Alexander once more to my bosom."

But her little Alexander, now twenty-one months old, took no notice of her when she swept into the nursery, arms outstretched to receive him. He sat among his wooden carts, more interested in the little girl on the floor beside him than in his mother. They could have been brother and sister. Both had flaming heads of tight golden curls. Both had the solemn eyes of the orphaned child that remembers neither mother nor father. The little girl was the child of Jean and Mathew McDonnell, the baby whom Mariota had taken from the croft at Auchtertipper to be reared in the castle. She was six months older than Alexander and, because she was a girl and had been longer there than he, she was cock of the roost. She decided on the games they were to play and he was her devoted slave. It was a dominance that continued throughout their childhood. He would build the giant's castle in the beech-tree and she would occupy it as the damsel in distress, to be rescued by him after a bloody fray with an invisible ogre. He would throw sticks up into hazel trees and gather the shiny olive brown nuts for her to make a necklace. Then at the age of seven she vanished from his life and for a while he was lost without her. She went back to Mathew 's croft to look after her father when Jean died bearing her second child. At that birth Mariota was powerless to save them. Following hours of torment a boy child was dragged dead from his mother's womb and minutes later her life fled with the blood from her exhausted body.

Fourteen

For children, Lochindorb was full of excitement and mystery. Alexander and Walter had been joined by James and Duncan and, almost as soon as they were weaned, each youngster found his devoted slave in the Hawk. Before they could walk, they were swung on to his broad shoulders, told to grab his thick eyebrows and carried to every part of the castle from the sculleries to the ramparts.

From the age of four each boy was expected to be able to ride. He was put in the care of the grooms who were ordered to get the lad on horseback. The horses used for the job were highland garrons, stocky hill-ponies with sure feet, wide backs and wicked habits, who would bite, toss and roll when they felt like it. The boys had to saddle these monsters themselves and rode barefoot, without stirrups so that they could come off quickly. Eventually the ponies accepted the youngsters, but it took a lot of patience and a great many falls. It was a method that made fine riders, for they were either good or good and dead!

Once they could ride, however, the lads found a freedom they had not dreamed of. To manage a horse skilfully was, to their father, the proof of their manhood and nothing was forbidden to them. Duncan, at the age of fourteen, became a bandit, feared even more than his parent. His hunting-ground was in the steep east-facing valleys that cut towards the carses and plains of Angus and Fife from the wilderness of the Grampians. Raiding the rich trade-roads between Aberdeen and Edinburgh so far from his home gave him independence and a captaincy he needed.

His older brothers Alexander and Walter channelled their youthful vigour differently. Alexander studied the art and craft of war. He became a sea-pirate and, later still, a mercenary in France before he won glory on the battlefield of the Red Harlaw, saving Scotland from ruin by his aunt's husband, MacDonald, the ambitious Lord of the Western Isles. Walter, studious thoughtful Walter, collected birds' eggs and butterflies and knew where to guddle a trout or trap a salmon and where to watch the red deer mating. Still in his teens, he laboriously catalogued the fauna and flora of Badenoch. Later, but still a young man, he was to fight desperately to preserve his inheritance in Wester Ross from the plundering of MacDonald's pirates.

He stood now at the edge of a steep slope, where firs encircled the valley of the Findhorn at Struie, and gazed across the flood-waters. The river, fed on snowmelt from the Monadhliaths, rubbed itself like a huge serpent against sandstone cliffs that twisted its shining black body into a rocky gorge before spewing it into the valley. The encircling firs, standing well back and wary of the river's power, were now lapped by its peat-dark waters. A thousand years of flood and check had carved cliffs and caverns in the rock, and in one hole, a horseman's height above the bracken, timber-wolves made a lair. Walter had studied their coming and going, examined their vomits and turds, watched them carrying their kills, rats and lambs, through the tangle of forest. He marked their lair by its nearness to an osprey's nest in a polled tree. The huge pile of sticks, green with moss, from which generations of birds had flown, made a reliable landmark in that swarthy forest of pine and juniper. He could see it now, a mile away, and by its relation to a dead tree across the valley he picked out the exact location of the wolf-lair. Down river, the waters were strangled into a gorge. Thus the valley lay, like an almond, surrounded by low cliffs and narrowed at each end by the river's throat. He looked down at the bowl of black water. He had never seen the Findhorn in such flood and was awed by the silent power of it.

"Well Walt, where are your wolves?"

Walter glanced down at the keen, sharp face of his younger brother and wished he had not boasted of his find. He had hoped to trap a wolf-cub later this year and tame it if he could. But James had got wind of his secret and wormed it out of him. James was not interested in studying the animals or in catching their young. Anything that moved was a target to be hunted to satisfy his lust for killing. That was why he was there on the brow of the hill with Walter and why, behind them, stood a small army of men armed with staves and swords.

"In a cave to the right of the osprey's tree there," Walter replied. Mind you, he thought, conditions would never be better for a hunt, for the flood denied the wolves several ways by which to avoid their pursuers.

"What we shall do," continued Walter, "is to smoke them out of their hole and drive them down the river-bank to where it narrows and where they can be cornered by the hounds."

James studied the scene. His quick imagination foresaw the kill. He and the dogs would be at the right spot awaiting the slinking brutes as they dodged from cover to cover.

"If we set alight the brushwood there," Walter pointed up river, "the wind will send the smoke directly into their hole. Your men must line the cliff from here downwards and move in on them with plenty of noise when I give the signal. MacVicar will come with me and when he dowses the smoke you will know that the wolves are on their way.

What he did not say was that if the wind changed and blew the fire towards the osprey's nest the game would be over. It was enough having to give up his ambition to catch a wolf-cub. He was determined this year to take an osprey chick and train it to the glove. He had a peregrine and a harrier, but his falconer had laughed at him when he talked of catching an osprey. "A fish-hawk my lord will never train, and will not stoop to a sparrow!" Falconery was in Walter's blood – his father loved the sport and had taught him well. The sight of those magnificent black and white fish-eagles flashing into a loch and carrying off a trout or a salmon made him long to possess one and prove the expert wrong.

"Come on then, what are you waiting for?" said James, who knew his brother had no interest in slaying wolves and that he had their father's support in mounting this hunt. James was impatient as usual.

"To begin with, the wolves may not be in their cave," replied Walter. "If they are, they will stay there long enough if they scent man. The fire must be started by the best stalker and that means by me. I don't trust any of those clumsy oafs to go near the lair." He called out to one of the waiting men, "MacVicar, you are good with fire. Take the tinderbox and come with me. But slowly and stealthily, mind! The rest of you spread out. James, take Duncan and the dogs as far down the valley as you can go and keep out of sight. You will be down-wind and if you are quiet and hidden the wolves will be up with you before they know you are there. They are quick and cunning, remember, and if they suspect danger they will break cover and attack!"

Walter and MacVicar, son of the priest, separated from the others and by a wide detour gradually approached the wolf-cave. They were now upwind of their quarry and despite their care it was not long before the head of the dog-wolf showed, nose high to the wind and sniffing their scent. Was he bigger than Walter remembered? Or was it fear that exaggerated his senses? They knelt behind a large upturned root-plate of a fallen tree and lit the fire. Old bracken and whin flared in sudden heat and pungent smoke stole down the path of the wind to the searching nose of the wolf. His hackles rose and he disappeared from sight. "Now, MacVicar, heap on the green stuff and really make a fug!" said Walter. Coughing, their eyes streaming, they followed the smoke towards the cave, thumping the ground with birch poles. When only a few yards from the lair they saw the two big beasts slink out and vanish downwind.

"Go back and dowse the fire," commanded Walter.

When the others on the brim of the flood-bowl saw the signal, they moved in, forming a straggle of men to the right of Walter that slowly and noisily drove the quarry towards the defile. The wolves had disappeared in deep bracken and broom and Walter knew they would not make themselves visible unless they found themselves trapped, when they would break through the beaters to freedom. When that happened, no man could stand in their path unharmed.

Slowly the shouting line of men converged towards the gorge. There was a distant yell of triumph from James. "I see them." Walter cursed his impetuous brother. Surprise was the essence of the hunt. Now the wolves would certainly know they were in a trap. Sure enough, a minute later there was a call from Duncan. "Quick, here they are." Then came a shriek, hoarse confused shouts from the beaters nearest to the hunters and the inhuman baying of the wolf-hounds as they leaped to the chase.

"Christ," swore Walter, "Duncan has been hurt," and ran as fast as he could, leaping over whin-bushes, struggling through shoulder-high bracken to where he had heard his young brother scream. "Bloody James!" He found himself swearing aloud. "He should never have given their position away." He came to a knot of men around a figure on the ground, broke through them and knelt beside the wounded man.

"James," he said in astonishment. "I feared it was Duncan."

A hard white young face glared up at him. "Well it is not your precious Duncan, it's me, James, that your damned wolf has savaged." The young man winced as his brother gripped his shoulder. "Fool," he yelled. "It's my chest the beast has torn." Blood oozed through his clothes.

"Quickly, men, make a litter and get him to the smith's bothy back there in the forest. MacVicar, take charge of my brother. You know best how to quench bleeding and salve a wound. You others, get after the hounds and keep Duncan away from the wolves. Your lord in Badenoch will be angered enough that one of his sons is hurt. Should two be mauled, there will be hangings!"

They carried James a mile up through the wood to the smith's croft. MacVicar showed his skill by binding his fist and plugging the wound in the boy's left breast, torn open by the wolf's jaws. MacVicar offered his flask of spirits. "Drink, Lord James, and bite on this piece of wood. Heat a dirk in yon forge, smith, till the point glows red." James shouted out, "You'll murder me, you brute," and struggled to free himself from the hands that held him to the litter.

"No, Lord James, but you will surely die if hot iron is not put to your wound. A wolf bite kills by inches but kills indeed and I have been told by Lord Walter to do what I must. Drink this, now." The glowing point of the dagger slid sizzling over the surface of the boy's chest, smoking, burning, purifying, and stopping the flow of blood. James screamed and fainted. "Bind him," said MacVicar. "Bind him tightly and lie him on his stomach. That way his weight will keep the wound dry and if he vomits it will not harm him."

Late that April night the hunting party returned to Lochindorb, Duncan with the bloody pelt of the dead dog-wolf across his young shoulders, James, pale but alive, on the litter. Walter had sent word ahead to warn the castle, and Mariota and Alexander Stewart were both at the watergate to help them off the boat.

"Look, Father," shouted Duncan and threw the skin of the dead wolf at his father's feet. Stewart nodded, patted the boy on the head. "Is James still alive?" he said, his deep voice threatening everyone. "Yes, Father," said the boy on the litter. Mariota threw her arms around him. "Christ, mother, take care." The wounded youth glared at her, looked expectantly up at his father. The latter pulled his cloak around him, turned and strode off into his fortress.

Fifteen

If in the nursery and in the saddle the boys and their parents were happy, it was sometimes otherwise in the hall and in the bedroom. Mariota's continuing position as Lady Lochindorb and mistress to Alexander Stewart was a perpetual annoyance to the King and an embarrassment to Alexander Bur the Bishop of Moray. King Robert blamed the bishop for failing to bring his unruly son in Badenoch to his senses and for that reason Bur lost no opportunity to remind Alexander Stewart of his wicked ways. That head-strong prince could thole no rebuke, but fretted at these gadfly pricks to his conscience. In the spring of thirteen eighty-two the vast territory of Ross came once more on the marriage market. Since her ill-fated betrothal to Alexander, Eufame had wed, by a strange trick of fate, one of the six Crusader Knights ransomed in 'seventy-four. But he, Sir Walter Leslie, was now dead and the riches of Ross were on offer again with their plump little countess. Since threats and scoldings had no effect on his son, the King tried bribery once more. If Alexander would give up this woman Mariota and marry Eufame not only would he, Alexander, be the superior to all lands north of the Firth but the King would make him justiciar with the authority of the throne at his command. Such an acquisition of power and property was not to be put aside by any man – certainly not by Alexander Stewart. He made his plans. He would be so wealthy that he could provide a castle in Buchan for Mariota where she would stay with the two youngest of their boys. He would cohabit with her when he wished but he would marry the Lady Eufame who would live with him at Lochindorb. Of course Mariota de Athyn would become a rich woman with an establishment equal to a countess. He would expect her to live a life of chastity for his sake and she might bear him a few more children if that pleased her.

It did not please her!

"You are locking me up in a gold-encrusted sty as if I were a breeding sow, to live a life of solitary sloth. Who will be my friends? No one. Who will come to visit me apart from you on a fornicating spree? No one. Why? Because no one would dare inflame the jealousy of the Earl of Buchan. Who will receive me in their homes? No one. Why? Because they would not wish to offend the bishop or the King by encouraging such a disreputable woman as Mariota, the Earl of Buchan's whore!" There was one huge, majestic row when she flung goblets, plates and even knives at the earl, who had to call in his men to seize her, or risk certain injury!

Nevertheless she was packed off to Castle King Edward beyond the river Spey and the river Deveron, a distance on foot from Lochindorb of nearly one hundred miles, for Alexander Stewart had left her no horse. Guarded by day and by night he made sure that his plans henceforth would be unopposed. Then, having cleared his decks of unnecessary cargo, he wasted no time in preliminaries and was wed to Eufame of Ross within a month. The lady had grown stout and, dispirited by a shortage of suitors, she had seized on Alexander's proposal with more haste than decorum. Bishop Bur, likewise, prepared himself to cut all corners, knowing that the King, who had sought this match for so many years, would not look kindly on delay.

When he had the Earl of Buchan on his knees before him at the high altar of the Cathedral in Elgin, Alexander Bur reminded him that fire and brimstone would be his lot if he renewed his fornicating ways. Stewart smarted under the lash. He swore to himself that he would visit King Edward Castle just as soon as he could free himself of the fusty stink of the bishop's vestments. More than that, he would make that parson sweat for daring to sermonise him at his wedding.

The marriage yoke that had been placed on Alexander and Eufame hung uncomfortably across their necks for exactly seven days and six nights. Alexander described his new wife as a "holy moaner who spent two hours on her knees before going to bed and when at last she climbed in beside me she was so well brought-up that she refused to remove her clothes!" Eufame convinced herself she had wed a coarse, dirty, demanding brute who lacked sensitivity and refinement. Stuck with each other, wedlock would have become deadlock. But on the seventh day Mariota arrived.

She had not feared Euphemia as a rival. She called her by her given name, Euphemia, and never addressed her by any other because she despised her. She was fat and quite unattractive. She dressed like a frump and simpered like a child. So when the news of the wedding reached her she was at first unbelieving and then extremely angry. She escaped from the castle by a simple expedient of inviting her gaolers to the table, filling them full of wine and ordering the Hawk to cut their throats. With the faithful dwarf, she procured horses by threatening the castle grieve and rode for the river Spey and the road to Grantown. She spent two nights on the way and she was fortunate that June of thirteen eighty-two was a warm sunny month, for to keep her journey secret she slept in a hillman's sheiling and in a ruined barn, wrapped up in a saddle-cloth. But at Castle Grant, a morning's ride from Lochindorb, she had an ally in Sir Robert, chief of the clan and recently appointed ambassador to the court of the King of France. Mariota counted him and his wife Matilda among her close friends and knew she could rely on them for hospitality and even for help, although Sir Robert would have some difficulty explaining to the King why he had been persuaded to assist her to usurp the position of the lawful wedded wife of the new Justiciar. But all she wanted at Castle Grant was a wash and a change of clothes. She had already made her plans and would not compromise her good neighbours in anything that might smack of conspiracy.

Next morning a knight, complete with cloak, plumed bonnet, boots and sword, took the hill road to Lochindorb, accompanied on foot by his squire, a tiny fellow, who wore a tight leather helmet that covered his bald earless head. Mariota was delighted with her disguise. Sir Robert quoted his favourite minstrel story and called her "a very parfit gentle knight", and Matilda, airing her French, kissed her on the cheek and wished her "bonne chance". In a mood of excitement and elation she rode from the castle through birch-woods starred with anemones. Clumps of primroses peeked at her from the young bracken and her "Hawk" padded along beside her. She had no clear idea what she was going to do once she entered her castle at Lochindorb but she knew that she was going to make something happen when she got there. "Hawk," she said, "when we arrive I want you to announce me as Mathew de Athyn. That is my brother's name and it will get me into the hall. Stay with me, but once I am in the presence of my lord Alexander and Lady Euphemia I do not think I will need your help!"

It was sunset when at last they looked down upon the loch. Mariota had never seen it so beautiful. The north was a blaze of colour where the sun rested briefly behind the far-away peaks of Ross and the hills of Sutherland. Her castle glowed like a jewel on a cushion of purple, then, when the dying sun touched the water, it appeared to float like a galleon on an ocean of amethyst and gold. A curlew called, plaintive, on the moor. A whisper of wind, rustling the heather, wiped the colour from the face of the loch. A dog barked in the castle – her dog, Brogach. Tears blurred her sight and she dashed them from her eyes. Never would another woman take control of her castle. Never would her man possess any other woman but her. The pony's ears pricked up at the sound of the barking dog and she dug her heels into its flanks. "Come, Hawk," she said, "I go now to claim my own."

Sixteen

Mariota stood in the middle of her Hall. Around her were the men and the women she knew and at the lord's table, raised to dignify those who supped above the salt, sat Alexander Stewart, Lady Euphemia, Murdo McInnes and her two older sons Sandy and Walter.

All heads turned to look at the young fellow who had entered so brazenly. They had heard the tiny squire announce the arrival of Mathew de Athyn, brother of the deposed lady of Lochindorb, but even before the master had made his reply – and he would have surprised everyone had he bidden the stranger enter – the youth strode boldly amongst them and placed himself not ten feet from the earl. He doffed his cap and bowed and his fair hair fell to his shoulders. Alexander Stewart looked coldly at the intruder.

A silence came over the noisy company as everyone guessed that something unusual was about to happen. "My lord earl." The young, clear, high voice reached through the Hall. "I have not ridden from beyond the Forth to be kept waiting at your gate, though no doubt it had been your intention to bar your doors on my unwelcome person. The new justiciar of the north is famed more for his dungeon than for his hospitality." He paused, awaiting the earl's response to this piece of insolence. The man in the high seat sat straight up. He gripped the table and glared at the speaker, black brows compressed in a scowl. "Continue," he said. "I am my sister's messenger, and perhaps her avenger also," said the young knight. "For eight years she has lived as mistress in this castle, your companion, bedmate, helper, and mother to your four sons, ever hopeful too that she might some day become your wife in the sight of God. And now you have abandoned her to feed your greedy ambition; imprisoned her in a castle far from here and taken to wife this creature, this nincompoop, whose only beauty and virtue is the length of her purse and the breadth of her territories, which matches the width of her backside! Sir, I am here to seek justice for my poor mal-treated sister. Rid yourself of this fat and ugly creature. Send her back to her fat and ugly mere. Restore Mariota to her rightful place in this castle and in your heart."

The shocked hush that followed this speech was shattered by the screams of the countess, assaulted by the insults. She turned, plum-red in the face, appealing to her husband. Suddenly the noise from her throat stopped. She brought her hand sharply to her mouth, faced her youthful tormentor, flung herself from her seat and stumbled, sobbing, from the Hall. The earl took no notice of her. He had not moved his eyes from the figure before him. As he stared, his look of unbelief changed to admiration. That was the look that had made Eufame pause, for the truth to break on her like a storm-wave on a sinking ship. Alexander Stewart gripped the table edge in both hands, swayed backwards on his seat and shook the rafters with a huge roar of laughter.

"Mariota! You are splendid! Magnificent! By Jesus, I have missed you. You are like a bolt from Cupid's bow compared to that imposter of a woman. By the Holy Grail, dressed in those breeches and boots you make me understand what it is the Arabians see in young boys! Come, my Titania, come. Your place is at my side. Offer me the Apothecary's Stone and I will not trade you for it! Look, your sons have recognised their mother. Rise, all you vassals, and welcome home my Mistress of Lochindorb!"

Mariota's victory was complete. The Countess of Ross left the very next day with her lapdogs yapping in her arms, and Alexander Stewart sighed a sigh of immense relief and satisfaction. He had done what his brother the King had desired, what old sticky-Bur the bishop had never expected – he had wed the heiress. He now had the territories of Ross to the north and to the west and, best of all, and without loss of face, he had Mariota. They could bluster, they could threaten, they could cajole, they could chastise, but he would never shift. She was his woman, the only woman to fill his spirit and his loins as well. By God, he felt younger and stronger already as he watched the countess and her retinue of young men, old maids and small dogs, bark and chatter their way across the water, out of his life, he hoped for ever.

Seventeen

Mariota 's return to her castle of Lochindorb heralded that part of her life which she was to consider the fairest adventure of all. Her life was filled with "adventures". She would awake of a morning as the early sunrise flashed over the mountain crests and turn her head to admire the homely, bearded face of her man as he lay, relaxed in sleep. She took care not to awaken him, for his carnal appetite was immense and she hated to feel used by any man, even by him. When she gave, she gave of her best, pouring our her love in the act of lovemaking, but she expected to receive as much in return, a fierce and total union of minds as well as of bodies. She knew that she could release, even from her fingertips, magic so powerful that, deep though his sleep might seem, her slightest touch would raise again that soft tassel to its magnificent glory. So she would lie awake, motionless in the thin light of dawn, and think. And the first thought to come to her as she hugged her knees under the soft eiderdown was, "I give thee thanks, O Holy Virgin Mary, protector of women, for the gift of love which thou hast laid upon me and for giving me the art to renew that gift as often as I wish with Alexander, my beloved." As she lay there, snug and naked, she reminded herself that she might not always be content with one man, no matter how skilfully and beautifully he aroused her. She had known others and she would know more. In love-making, as with all pretty things, it was by comparing what was hers with what others had that excited her pride of possession.

Her present "adventure" had started with the routing of the Countess of Ross and was so idyllic that she almost wished it would end lest she be turned into a complacent cow like some of her friends, pampered by their husbands, fat and lazy like Euphemia's lapdogs. But her lord, Alexander, made it his rule not to indulge her, and the gains, little or large, that she wrested from life had been won by careful planning and sometimes, but not too often, by brazen importuning. On such occasions she hated herself a little, although it was fun and she knew that he enjoyed the play as much as she. Loch-an-Eilean, for instance, had been won only by the most blatant seduction!

She had fallen in love with the tree-girt loch that hid itself so well among the mountains. Everything in that enchanted place, the birches that glittered green in the spring, pure gold in the autumn and purple against the snow, the still, black water that mirrored mountains and trees, and especially the lonely little island, made her heart ache and her spirit soar. From the first time that she had ridden into the valley with Alexander one warm July afternoon she knew that she wanted to possess it. The island captivated her by its silence, by its nearness and by the mystery of its blackened heap of stones that had once been a hermit's hut. She had heard the story of Hamish Shaw, who lived there years ago, and knew that Loch-an-Eilean had become part of the legend that was beginning to grow around her husband, the justiciar.

Hamish Shaw had been a solitary man who worked on farms, in the forest and at the mason's trade, in return for enough food to live on and enough drink to dull his perceptions and blur his visions. He had been half-brother to Seath Mor, champion swordsman of the clan Ay, but he was cursed by the possession of the second-sight. Death was his companion, the horrid figure that stood always behind him, whispering, how that man would meet his end and when this one would die. Rumour of his strange power spread like floating dandelion-seeds and, like them, his predictions took root. At first some men and many women sought to use his clairvoyance to their advantage. A son would seek him out to learn if he had long to wait for his inheritance. An ill-used wife unexpectedly acquired patience when she was told that she would outlive her brutal husband. But one day Hamish Shaw was moved by an uncontrollable compulsion to foretell the fates of those who sought to use him and he became the loneliest of men. He built a shelter on the little island in the loch where only the wagtails and the brown-headed gulls were his friends, and tried to quench with uisge beatha the ungodly fire that flamed inside him and which made him speak with the voice of the Reaper.

Then he disappeared and the superstitious hill-people believed he had been carried off to Hell by a water-kelpie. Others said that the Devil in the guise of a great black boar had come upon him, drunk at Aviemore, and had champed him with its slobbering jaws bit by bit, until not one small piece of gristle remained. But because his coracle was still there, tied to a tree on his island, others declared they had seen a monstrous eagle swoop upon the hermit's hut and soar up into the clouds carrying in its talons the pluck of a man. No one ventured across the water to prove that tale true, until, to put an end to these and other beliefs that had turned the Clan Shaw into a gabble of old women, the justiciar himself put it to the test.

"Have any of you ever seen a sow or a boar eat a man? No! Have you seen an eagle rip out the heart and lungs from any living creature your own size? Your tales are rubbish. Your stories, and your beliefs in them, make you less than men and I will not have a pack of whimpering dogs as my neighbours. Give me a boat and with McInnes here I shall go to your hermit's island. No doubt I shall find that he died from starvation, since not one of you was man enough to give him bread!"

The truth was less romantic than the tales, but no less horrible. The Earl and his lieutenant found the body of Hamish Shaw in his hut, half-eaten by vermin and crawling with maggots. As they pushed open the door the sweet, foul stench of putrefaction made them gasp and they had scarcely time to take in the havoc when fat feasting blue-bottles rose in a buzzing cloud on to their faces.

"Ugh," exclaimed Alexander Stewart and made for the door, hand over his mouth. "McInnes, if we move this stinking corpse it will fall to pieces. We shall fill this hovel with wood and all the tinder we can collect, dried gorse will make a good blaze, and roast everything."

They heaped driftwood, bracken, dead whin, inside the hut, pulled down the turf roof and set it all alight, with what was left of Hamish Shaw at the heart of the fire. But by destroying one myth the justiciar had created another. The pall of smoke that rose above the tree-tops was seen by the hill-folk as a demon, an ogre or a bear, and some of the mystical power of the dead seer was transferred by the men and the women of Rothiemurchus and Glenmore to the person of Alexander Stewart of Lochindorb.

When Mariota first saw the island on its loch it was the peace and the exquisite beauty of the place that claimed her attention and not the near-forgotten story of the death of Hamish Shaw. In her mind's eye she saw a fortalice on the island which, for Alexander and herself, would be a haven from the problems and distractions of their lives at Lochindorb. Shamelessly she set about convincing her man of his need for such a retreat and of the joys of having such a place in this lonely and lovely glen. Of course, she succeeded. Within a week, masons were hired from Elgin and men were detailed to prepare the site and to build a castle in Loch-an-Eilean. It was to be a small castle – a fortalice as Mariota had suggested. Like his fortress at Lochindorb it would cover the entire island, with an outer wall that rose sheer from the loch. Boatloads of hewn stone were ferried across the narrows on rafts and the justiciar himself took his household to Ruthven Castle, not far away, to supervise the work.

As befitted his position as King's deputy he travelled always with a retinue and one day he was seated on horseback at the water's edge with his guard, his sons and his servants. They were watching the last load of rubble and squared stone being loaded on to a builder's raft, when they heard the sound of a horn in the forest behind them. Soon after, a hunting party appeared among the pines with a large stag slung across the back of a garron.

"A good day to you and God be with you, Earl."

A man about Stewart's age walked his horse out of the wood towards the shore. He wore a flat green velvet cap; a black linen tunic covered his leather jerkin and on it, embroidered in gold, was the coat-of-arms of the Bishop of the Province of Moray.

"Bishop Alexander Bur," Stewart replied courteously enough. "What brings you a-hunting so far from home, and in my forest? Has your pursuit of that fine beast I see, obliged you to forget, in the excitement of the chase, your obligation to inform me of your intentions?"

Bur's heavy-jowled face became grim. "My lord of Buchan, that question shall with greater justice be directed at your own activities. Can it be that you are not aware, you, the justiciar of the north, that this is my land, church land, that you are unlawfully building upon?"

A heron flapped heavily from a reed-bed and wheeled up the loch to find a more peaceful stance.

"I advise you, Bishop," said Stewart slowly, "to follow the example of that bird and take yourself back to the safety of your cloisters before the hawk swoops. I know well that you claim title to a great part of the Strath of Spey over which you and your church have no right whatever. To extend the pretence and to include in your ambitions the very heart of Badenoch is to take the matter beyond my patience."

"I make no claim, my lord. This land belongs to me," said the bishop, his voice raised in annoyance.

"Then present your proof to my court," retorted the justiciar bluntly and with an equal show of anger.

Bishop Bur scowled at his adversary, wheeled his horse and rode off with his party. Alexander Stewart moved not a muscle until he had vanished from sight among the forest undergrowth, then he turned to his men, smote his knee and exclaimed, "God's blood! I'll have that fat churchman stuffed and served on my supper-table. How much patience am I expected to have? How far must I control myself in front of that sour-faced priest? Come men, let us complete the building of my castle on my island in my loch in the heart of my country – Badenoch, and damned be Bur and all his greedy lot!"

Eighteen

To the justiciar's court in the heart of Badenoch came Bishop Alexander Bur of the Provence of Moray, whose spiritual authority extended with his lands as far as the diocese of Aberdeen and marched with the See of Ross. He made the wearisome journey from his cathedral in Elgin armed with his papers, and a determination to put the justiciar in his place. Their meeting at Loch-an-Eilean had not been an accident. For as long as the Bishop had enjoyed his Bishopric, Stewart had been Lord of Badenoch. Stewart was five years younger than Bur but the latter considered the justiciar less than half of his intellectual age – a young whipper-snapper who had been handed too much power too soon by his father the King. A justiciar in his twenties! What folly! A man who could not control his passions should not have half of Scotland in his keeping. The bitterest pill that Bur had had to swallow was the farce that Alexander Stewart had made of his marriage. When clearly warned of the hellfire that awaited him should he disregard his bishop's advice, the Lord of Badenoch had taken his whore Mariota to bed with him only a week or so after he, the bishop, had solemnized his wedding to the Countess of Ross.

The bishop rode south to Kingussie and to the justiciar's court prepared to take a very firm stand against this sinful prince. He was surprised and even pleased by the courtesy accorded to him at Ruthven Castle and not least by the very ample board which sagged under its load of cooked meat and fish and fowl. After days in the saddle and nights of unease when he had been obliged to sleep in places unfitting his dignity and far removed from the comforts of his palace at Spynie, he was encouraged by the lavishness of his reception. Indeed, he had begun to alter his opinion, slightly, of his adversary. Confident that his own case was unassailable, he had even considered modifying the hard line he intended to pursue by adding just a modicum of conciliation. Words were all that Bishop Bur ever gave away.

But that was before he left Ruthven Castle for the justiciar's court at Kingussie. His host had insisted that he and his party precede him from the castle and the bishop had not been slow to accept this honour as being his due. He was ferried across the Spey and by mischance, as was explained to him, "because of the flood" – although he could see no sign of flooding – the boat had grounded half a mile downstream on a mud-flat. He and his company then plodded through a marsh to reach a knoll on which they saw the tenting of many pavilions. But when they gained the summit they found themselves not on the hill of the Standing Stones of Easter Kingussie, the ancient Druid-hallowed site of the justiciar's court, but on an adjacent hilltop separated from the other by a steep gully. The tents he had seen were only a foil.

Muddied and angry, Alexander Bur eventually took his place before a smiling Alexander Stewart who looked down on him from his justiciar's throne and enquired what had kept him! Then, without waiting for a reply, the earl declared that since the bishop had wasted half of the day getting there he could therefore allow him only a limited time to state his case. In addition, he decreed that, although the subject of the legal titles could be debated, there could be no disputing the Forest Rights of the justiciar who had the sole privilege of hunting deer, stag, wolf, boar and bear in lands where he represented the King. He directed that Bishop Bur, by taking a stag without his authority, was guilty of transgressing the Forest Laws. The penalty, as all knew, was death. However, continued the justiciar, he wished to show goodwill and clemency and would restrict the penalty to a fine of one hundred gold merks to be paid over at the end of the sitting.

Proceeding to the more serious debate on land rights he invited the bishop to lay before the court his proof of the title he had assumed to

75

lands in Badenoch. The bishop protested that the imposition of a time-limit was no way to conduct such important business, and was instructed to proceed or withdraw.

Following Alexander Bur's submission, Stewart announced that because he, the Earl of Buchan, being also the Lord Justiciar, was a party to the case, he himself could not intervene, but had placed the onus of refuting the bishop's claim on the master of rolls, brought north from the seat of government and well versed in those matters in dispute. Compeared that person, commissioned to attend, a euphemism for the substantial bribe paid to this weak man who subsisted on patronage! He spoke at length and produced documents which Bur suspected were fictitious, yet which he was powerless to dispute, documents that established Stewart's claim not only to all the lands twixt Lochindorb and Ruthven but to every rood and furlong in the Strath of Spey from Laggan to the Gar-mouth. This was a very great blow to the churchman. "If this pirate has his way," thought the bishop, "there will be loss of revenue from all the small ecclesiastical foundations that I have visited this week and censured for their lack of provider. And, here was the crux, the salmon catch at the mouth of the river was at peril, which, by lease or by let, swells the coffers of the Provincal Church not inconsiderably." He remonstrated. The authority for his fishing-rights was by an Act of King David I concerning the church lands and revenues in Moray. The justiciar shook his head. His proof was incontrovertible and lay in the Archives of the Registry. He judged the bishop's case unproved and fined him the costs of the hearing.

"Out of consideration for your age I invite you to stay the night at my castle at Ruthven or in my fortalice in Loch-an-Eilean. You may, of course, consider that too much of your time has already been spent, fruitlessly, here in Badenoch, and wish to return home. It is your choice."

The day was far spent. Rainclouds filled the eye of the wind. Either the bishop spent a dismal and wet night in the forest at the mercy of its wolves, or he could rest dry and alive in the lair of that other wolf, whom he recognised now and belatedly as his scheming and implacable foe. Rain spattered on the tenting and a cold blast filled the justiciar's pavilion. With a poor grace, Bishop Bur accepted the comfort of Ruthven Castle.

Nineteen

Mariota knelt before the statue of Christ; Jesus in oak; Jesus smooth, glowing, polished by a thousand hands; Jesus dying; Jesus in all the strength of his manhood; Jesus crucified. It was midday. Light filled the tiny room, flowing from the white sky, rippling in sharp spears from the shining face of the loch, flooding and flashing through two small arched windows under the battlements. She loved this little space high in the sky. Its bare stonework was unadorned. There were no furnishings save the two embroidered cushions on which she knelt, a small table to take her arms, and the wooden Jesus. Here, He looked out over water and pine-forest to the eternal hills.

"I will lift up mine eyes unto the hills from whence cometh my help. My help cometh from the Lord which made both Heaven and earth."

There was one other statue she loved and revered just as much, but it hung in another room, her bedroom, in front of her four-poster which was a replica of Queen Eleanor's marriage bed, canopied in tapestry, draped with silks, covered with transparent figured lace, the bed where already a child had been conceived – God grant it be a girl. That statue watched over her as she joined with her man, as he plunged inside her, as she rode him like a Boadicea until her nails drew blood from his shoulders, or as she lay warm, happy, exhausted in his arms. And always the Virgin Mary with the child Christ at her breast, protector of women, looked down upon her. Mariota giggled. She watched with a little envy perhaps? Alexander had a name for their bed. Since he had returned one night, earlier than she expected him and found his place taken by her two favourite hounds, he had called it her Ark.

As yet he had no by-name for this little chapel and she hoped he never would. His humour now was often harsh and as brutal as his way of living. She remembered how proud she had been of him, when he had thwarted the bishop and protected his rights and especially her dear little Loch-an-Eilean. She had known in her heart that his victory would not last, that the stubborn churchman would not meekly go home, and she had been right.

For two years Alexander Stewart, justiciar, squeezed the money-bags of Bishop Bur. He slapped a tax on all church property in his territory and with a small army of highland caterans he made sure that the dues were paid in full. His legal plundering was performed in the King's name and, when the gold started to tinkle into the royal coffers, the bishop's complaints fell on deaf ears. Stewart had to pay and feed his mercenaries and, to do this, raiding the trade routes had become Lochindorb's chief business. Beyond the Monadhliath mountains lay the Great Glen of Albyn, the chief highway between Moray and Ross and the Western ocean. Through this glen passed rich merchandise exchanged for the salt beef, salmon, hides and timber of the northern provinces, merchandise which included silks and swords from Iberia, linens from the low countries, icons, vessels of gold and silver, and richly ornamented vestments on their way to monasteries, kirks and cathedrals of the dioceses in the east and north. One successful attack could clean out a baggage-train and pursuit was impossible in the wilderness of mountain and bog between Glen Albyn and Lochindorb. By the many gifts he brought back to her, from the whispered exchanges of the women and from the boasting of men, Mariota knew that her justiciar, like her son Duncan, had become robber. The raids became bloodier. Some men did not return. There was weeping of wives and sweethearts and Mariota prayed fervently that she would never have to weep as they did.

Then in the early light of a summer's morning he came home wounded. His left shoulder was a bloodied mess transfixed by an arrow. The barb was bedded in his joint, its broken shaft protruding from his jerkin. Tight-lipped, pale, he reached the castle unaided.

Mariota was told that he had been hit five hours before and had ridden forty painful miles.

They cut his clothes from him, warmed him in heated skins and filled him with hot spirits. Only then did McInnes, his henchman, draw his long sgiandubh, roast the point in fire and dig out the barb. Biting on a wad of leather, the earl, deadly pale, made no sound, as hot, Stockholm tar was poured on to the bleeding and mutilated shoulder and bound tight. It was months before he could mount a horse and his arm never regained its strength. He was in constant pain and swore loudly and often at his servants and at his family.

Far from being a disaster, the raid, on treasure salvaged from a wrecked ship off the Moray coast, had yielded the greatest prize of all and in the smith's forge a pair of massive candlesticks and two baptismal bowls were melted down. The ingot provided a year's work for a goldsmith who fashioned plates and goblets for the earl's table. For Mariota, he made the golden snake with clasps fashioned as wildcats, that hung from her neat waist to the vee of her thighs and glinted wickedly, like the serpent in the Garden of Eden.

That picture of the wicked Serpent, of Eve and the apple, was one of her most loved illustrations in her "Book of Hours".

When the Wolf was away – and she never knew whether it was on lawful business or banditry – Mariota would retreat into her tiny church to seek forgetfulness in the ritual of religious observance. Her companion there was her Book of Hours. The calf-bound volume was a gift from Queen Eleanor after their miraculous escape from the castle of St Hilarion. When deliverance came, the Queen, haunted so long by the nearness of death, pressed jewels on the three Scotswomen who by their determination helped her to survive. To Mariota she gave her Book of Hours. It had been copied, she said, from the Book of Hours presented to Queen Jeanne d'Evreaux by King Charles of France and engraved by the original artist and illuminator. The little book was the most precious thing that Mariota had. Nothing she owned was so beautiful; the soft cream calf of the binding, so delicate to touch and so comforting; the vellum pages, each with its text in black gothic script and biblical scenes illuminated in red and in gold, wafer-thin and transparent.

She knelt before the Christ, the Book open at her favourite picture, the Annunciation, with Archangel Gabriel and Mary in Mary's little house. The angel's wings gleamed silver, the tiles on Mary's roof were of azure blue. The Virgin's dress fell in soft silken folds from her head and her shoulders, a crimson halo shone around her face and she blushed in a most becoming way with pleasure and surprise. From lauds to compline the pictures differed. Always there was something Mariota had not noticed before – little figures in a corner, shepherds with their crooks and their placid sheep. She turned the pages slowly. Here was the mystery of the Incarnation; there, the terror on the faces of the Holy Family as they fled to Egypt from Herod and his child-killers. Her little book was an invitation to her to spend more and more time on her knees. What a dull place this would be without it, she thought. Every twelvemonth she had either just conceived or was about to give birth. Five sons followed each other into Lochindorb. Now, she prayed to the Virgin Mary and Archangel Gabriel that she might bear a girl-child. Boys were useful. Girls demanded dowries. As long as he was filling her with sons, Alexander Stewart would find no reason to cry, cease!

Twenty

The new baby, a girl, praise be to Mary, was scarcely crawling when Bishop Bur reopened his attack on the Lord of Badenoch and Buchan. Early one morning a monk rode to the shore of Lochindorb and was ferried to the castle. The earl and his family had gathered for breakfast when the man entered the hall. He was garbed and cowled in black. He bowed to Stewart, took a parchment from the folds of his cloak and handed it to him. No word was spoken, for the visitor's uncompromising austerity had silenced the room. He stood like a statue, only his pale hands showing beyond the shroud, his face invisible. The earl tossed the roll to Mariota.

"Acquaint me with whatever is of importance in this fustian," he said. Mariota broke the seal, scanned the script carefully and spoke at last.

"You are commanded, my lord, to appear before the bishop's synod to answer certain charges and condemnation, under pain, my lord, of excommunication."

Mariota dropped her voice to a whisper as she spoke. Of all judicial punishment meted out by the Church, excommunication was the most fearful. Torture, burning at the stake, which was the fate of the heretic, was less abhorrent than the sentence that condemned a man's soul to toss for ever in purgatory.

In silence, the earl studied the figure before him. "You know what is written here?" The black head bowed a fraction.

"Then if you are not a villain you are a fool, or a brave man." He paused. "It is customary to show respect when approaching the justiciar. Hawk. Bare this man's head so that I can gain the measure of him." The dwarf moved fast but the man in black was even faster. With a sweep of one hand he threw back the cowl and with the other pinioned the Hawk's arm.

"Ask and it shall be given. I do not relish coercion," he said.

He now stood bareheaded before the justiciar and, of a sudden, a shadow had become a man, and a man to be reckoned with. His young, clean-shaven face was topped by a full head of tousled black hair, and eyes that gave nothing held the earl's in a hard stare. No one in the room moved. The earl leaned back in his chair and spoke, slowly and thoughtfully.

"You are young, you are strong. You are no monk. What manner of cub does Bishop Bur send to beard the Wolf in his den?" He laughed. "I know right well the name you give me. The Wolf of Badenoch. My God, Bur has a nerve to command the Wolf to do his bidding. And you, whoever you are, you, whom he has chosen to act as messenger, you, I could flay alive this very morning, or slowly drown in the Water Dungeon beneath this Hall." His right hand came up and touched his left shoulder. "If this damned wound was healed I would have wrestled with you myself – for the simple joy of laying you on your back. So silent? Have you nought to say for yourself?"

The man had not taken his eyes from him and, when he spoke at last, his voice surprised everyone by his meekness.

"The wickedness in your life has led you by a dangerous road, my lord Justiciar. Had you not attacked the bishop and the Holy Church, you would not now be suffering pain in your arm or in your heart. I believe that you will bring yourself to the Cathedral at Elgin, in humility and in penitence, for you have no other way to turn. May God forgive you and have pity on your soul."

He bowed and strode quickly from the Hall. As the door closed behind him the spell he had cast suddenly snapped. Two chairs crashed as two of Stewart's sons jumped to their feet. Alexander, the older, vaulted the table and made to rush after the monk.

"Stay, Sandy," ordered his father. "No good can come of that. Let the viper go.

"He dared to preach at you like a schoolmaster to a wayward child and you say, let him go! "exclaimed Walter. "Kill him, Father, or I shall!"

83

"Enough of that. There will be no killing. This is Bur's work. And it is to Bur I shall address myself. That plaguy churchman shall trip over his fine vestments and I will be there to help him with a push!" He laughed and turned to Mariota. But she had not even heard him. She stared at the door through which the young man had passed.

"Mariota," Stewart said.

"My lord?" She saw his look and flushed.

"Do you not regret, my lord, that such a man should become a monk?"

Twenty-one

Assembled in the Cathedral in Elgin was the most impressive and glittering array of prelates ever seen in Scotland outside the Abbey of Arbroath where the Kings were crowned. Under the threat of excommunication – the direst sentence that Rome could pass – the earl attended the bishop's synod. Mariota was not there, of course, but her faithful Hawk described to her the splendour, the pomp, the dignity, of the occasion and also the devastating effect it had on her lord. For, confronted by this most powerful assembly of the Holy Church – bishops not only from their sees in Scotland but from Sodor, from England, and even from France – the earl's arrogance was subdued. He publicly burned his papers of proof and admitted the bishop's rule, spiritual and temporal, over the sweet lands of Spey. But he retained all Badenoch. The Hawk reckoned that Alexander Bur knew that only more trouble would come of pressing that claim.

It had indeed been the bishop's day and he squeezed every ounce of satisfaction from it, for the defeat of the justiciar meant more to Bur than the acquisition of land. In that predatory prince, as Bur described him, he had recognised a grave threat to his power. The Earl of Buchan was the King's son and, when King Robert died, which might be soon, would be the new King's brother. Already he had whetted the royal appetite with the bishop's gold, and kings above all others were possessed by the greed of Midas. Defiance of Holy Law amounted to heresy and there was enough of that about in Europe for the contagion to spread, unless the rule and the authority of the Church was undisputed. Also, its wealth was the envy of a monarchy impoverished by years of war with England and fratricide at home. The Church is like a dripping roast before a beggar, thought Bur, and beggars had a habit of becoming brigands. Well, he had vanquished one such brigand. Let others take heed!

In his fortress in Lochindorb the Wolf licked his wounds. He had to admit to himself, if to no other, that he had been cowed – he knew no man who would not have been, under such a dire threat – and that his bravado had vanished like a summer hailstorm. His pride had been pricked. He knew it and he resented the bishop's victory mainly on that account. He had lands enough in Moray, Buchan and Ross without Strathspey. But beyond and above the humiliation, a ragged red devil had begun to rage. Mariota had changed. His hurt pride made him quick to recognise it. Ever since Bur's envoy had stared him out and delivered his master's ultimatum, Mariota had changed. He remembered her words that morning and, even more, her look. When he returned from Elgin the eagerness had still been there, but now it had gone and he knew she had withdrawn from him in some subtle way. When spoken to, she replied with her usual directness, but more as a stranger than as a lover should. A thin veil spread itself between them and behind that veil waxed the little red demon in his soul. And so, in the months that followed, the worm of humiliation was joined by the snake of jealousy. His temper, never controlled, now blazed. Men and women stayed clear of him and, with loneliness, came the insidious hatreds that confounded judgement. The castle became a sullen, fearful place as men were punished for crimes they scarce had thought on.

Among all his acquaintances, sons, friends and servants, Murdo McInnes alone, the black-jowled long-haired captain of his highland army, could speak with him freely without fearing the consequences. It was Murdo who recognised his master's malaise and sought to divert his bruised and brooding spirit to more profitable objectives. He came to him one evening and spoke of what he knew of Bishop Bur. He told him how detested he was by poor and rich alike. He had been told, said Murdo, that none but those from whom their bishop sought advantage were permitted to enter his cathedral and how 'the greater the gift the greater the pardon' had become a byword in the Provence. Alexander Bur had surrounded himself with indecent wealth. T'was time, some said, that the golden candlesticks, the silver orbs and the icons with rubies and precious stones were put to better use.

"By the Lord Jesus," exclaimed Stewart, "I declare the fat churchman sleeps cosily in his golden cocoon, and feeds on swanflesh and French wines, while the poor clamour unheeded and the unshriven dead lie heaped in his charnel-houses. I shall scourge these porcine priests and bleed them white. McInnes, mount me a crusade against the villainous Bur. My God! I will make him smart and rue the day he ever clapped eyes on the Wolf of Badenoch!"

Twenty-two

The Wolf's "army" of caterans was recruited from the herdsmen of the crofts of the Dulnain, the Duthil and the Dorback, small fertile glens that grew oats, and kale in the winter, and supported a population of hillfolk, herdsmen and hunters. Alexander Stewart was as aware as any feudal lord who held fief from the King of his obligations to raise a levy of men trained for war from the serfs in his domain. His preference however was not for hundreds of reluctant conscripts torn from their farms and their families, but for a few score loyal and willing men of proved efficiency and courage. He made sure of these by "planting" them in the black houses of the small glens which cut into his moors and mountains near Lochindorb. There they could settle their wives, breed their bairns and rely on his munificence to survive the hard long winters when their cattle and sheep were long since slaughtered and eaten. Then they became his huntsmen, gleefully plundering among the vast herds of red deer that descended from the snow to find winter feed in the royal forest of Lennoch and in the bishop's forest of Rothiemurchus. The latter, in the mountain bowl north of the Cairngorms, provided shelter and grazing among its ancient pines for thousands of deer, red and roe, and, since Bur's hesitation in asserting his claim to Loch-an-Eilean, was the richest source of meat to the Lord of Badenoch. The men of the crofts sold their skill at arms to their master for his meal, his whisky and enough deer-meat to feed their families until the summer came again. Fifteen score, boys of fourteen to men of fifty, was the number Murdo McInnes could command at the rallying-point in the forest by the loch's shore. The raids in Glen Albyn were usually accomplished by fifty men with back up support and horses, and the caterans who descended with Duncan from Glen Prosen to cut the traffic at Forfar or Brechin required two supply camps between the east coast and Lochindorb. The trade between Aberdeen and Perth was lucrative and the spoils well worth the cost of the organisation.

Now the Lord of Badenoch had a different target and a very particular aim. Often he had cursed Bishop Bur and swore he would make him sweat. Now he planned to make him fry, and frizzle like a fat trout on a bogwood fire. The Wolf's objective was Elgin, a town of turf and wattle surrounding the royal castle on its hill, and its one hundred and fifty-year-old cathedral that was the pride of the bishopric and the so-called Lantern of the North. This magnificent house of God stood on a green haugh of the river Lossie, half a mile east of the castle, and around it clustered the manses of the canons and of the precentor, the deanery, the church of Greyfriars, the hospital of the Maisondieu and, nearer to the castle than the rest, the monastery of the Blackfriars. There was no other square mile north of Perth that could yield such plunder. Several ornaments in gold and in silver intended for the cathedral had already changed their shape in the forge at Lochindorb. Stewart knew that the pillage of church property would fill his coffers and, he hoped, buy off the fiercest condemnations from the King's Court. He listened, therefore, with attention to Murdo McInnes as he revealed his plan. First it would be Forres, twelve miles from Elgin, where the archdeacon lived and where his church was, and in May thirteen hundred and ninety both went up in flames, together with a large part of the town.

The Fiery Purge had begun and it brought an instant reaction from the bishop. The Bull of Excommunication was called down on Alexander Stewart, justiciar, which not only cut him off from the Holy Church but laid a duty on all Christian men to stop, if necessary to slay, this rabid Wolf of Badenoch. Bishop Bur had wasted no time. He knew how effective the mere threat of excommunication had been and, like Daniel in the lion's den, he felt confident that through faith and the immense power of the church he could render his adversary harmless. But, just in case, he ordered mass to be sung round the clock and drew up an emergency plan, should power and prayer both fail. If with these measures Alexander Bur felt secure, few others in the cathedral shared his confidence.

The mood at Lochindorb three days after the attack on Forres was quite different from the fear and dejection that engulfed the religious houses in Elgin, and at Pluscarden, the priory of the Cistercians between Forres and Elgin. Despite wholesale destruction, little of value had been taken from the burnings – a dozen pewter jugs, an icon and a few Forres maidenheads. It had only been a rehearsal for the next raid, and to kindle the enthusiasm of his men the Wolf arranged for a great feast to take place in the castle.

It was early summer. The pastures by the mountain streams were black with young cattle and on the high slopes sheep and longhorned red steers grazed with their cows on their favourite grasses. A dozen prime stots were slaughtered, quartered, roasted, and Stewart threw open the castle hall for his serfs and their families to fill their stomachs with his beef and ale. They came by the boatload, timid at first, then, as the hot ale worked in them, the crowded hall became bedlam. The Wolf, Mariota and their children, with McInnes and one or two others honoured to sup above the salt, sat on the raised platform at the end of the room, nearest to the kitchens from whence they were served with the choicest cuts of meat and with the ruby wine of France. The noise was earsplitting as the people below, intent on getting their share, and more, hacked at the hot beef, fought for the crisp fat and the well-browned outer pieces. Dogs vied with children for the ribs that were thrown to them and lapped up the beer left forgotten in tankards on the floor.

No one saw, or bothered to remark on, the black-garbed stranger who elbowed his way through the crowd, edged sideways along the wall and reappeared on the dais behind the principals. All, his family, Mariota and especially Stewart himself, were drunk by now and were enjoying the spectacle of men and women ogling each other, slapping each other, as, sated with food and liquor, they enjoyed freedom they seldom knew and a conviviality quite absent from their drab lives. The beer sparked lust in the men and drowned the inhibitions of the women. Some had freed their plump paps to the mouths of their swains. Some lay together on the floor, clasped in private oblivion among the snarling dogs and the shrieking children. The lord and his lady swayed on their seats, rocking with laughter. The boys, who had never seen such a spectacle, flung questions at their parents and comments to each other that raised gales of mirth from their elders.

The stranger stood behind them and watched. Then he leaned over between Alexander and Mariota and said, loudly enough to be heard by both above the din:

"Your time is nigh, my lord of Badenoch. Look well, for Hell cannot be unlike this. I bear the missive that condemns you to Purgatory. Laugh on! You will laugh little at the end!"

Drunk as he was, the Wolf recognised the voice and turned to seize the speaker, but the stranger eluded him and continued:

"This, Earl of Buchan, is the last word you shall have from the Holy Church. This, is your nemesis! "He drew out the Bull of Excommunication and laid it in front of Mariota.

"Read it to him, lady. Every word shall burn his soul, as Forres burned."

Mariota looked into a pale earnest face, saw the intense eyes and the wisp of dark, curly hair that fell over his cheek. She heard Alexander Stewart roar out. She saw him rise to seize the stranger and, without hesitation, she cast herself in an apparent swoon, against his chest. In a trice, the man had gone, vanished, in the tangle of bodies, arms and legs that swayed and sang and swayed and fell, heedless to everything, even to the shouts of their Lord of Badenoch.

Twenty-three

June of thirteen hundred and ninety was hotter than old men could remember. Streams still chuckled and gurgled from distant tarns that had gathered snow-water in spring, but they were poor, starved relations of the white torrents that had bearded the mountains and leapt and splashed between emerald banks of moss only a month before. The heather was dull and brittle, broken, brown before its time, and the woods with their tangle were tinder-dry. A cloud of smoke, far to the west, marked a forest fire that would crackle and dance over mile upon mile of birch and pine till it died on the dead moor. As if to protect its land, a sea-fog drifted in as evening came, blotting out hills and valleys, drenching all in white beads of dew. With the first pale rays of morning it stirred, then fled, fearful of the day, leaving a landscape glistening with spiders' webs on which the sunbeams split themselves in sharp spears of brilliant light.

Murdo McInnes left Lochindorb before dawn. When he reached the loch of the Romach and followed the Black Burn into the vale of Pluscarden, he overtook the coastal haar creeping back to the Firth. He pulled his cloak around him and urged his horse to a canter to escape the graveyard chill of the woods. He rode past fields and orchards and an occasional white-robed monk, bent among his cabbages. Pluscarden Abbey loomed through the mist and the Matins bell rung sharp and clear. He skirted the low boundary wall, noting the height of the windows, the grotesque faces of the gargoyles, the lofty timber roofs and the straggle of thatched farm buildings tucked behind, among the woods on the hill of the Wangie. Murdo smiled. He could forsee no opposition here and the buildings would burn well. He splashed his horse through the river Lossie at Palmers' Cross and reined in atop the small knoll that overlooked the walled town of Elgin.

In the castle, folk were stirring. Smoke drifted from its kitchens and below its grey walls it oozed through thatched roofs of a hundred small stone-and-wattle houses. These sat back from the road and had been built on either side of the ridge that ran straight as a die for half a mile to the cathedral. From his vantage-point, McInnes could see clearly into the church precinct. Smoke showed where the manses were and the hospital of Maisondieu. Breakfast had begun in the town of Elgin. North of him, rigs of yellow barley and golden corn scarred the green crook of land that bordered the river and between these and the precentor's house he could see the busy waterwheel of the bishop's mill. He counted aloud on his fingers: "Eighteen manses, the castle-house of the precentor, the Greyfriars church and monastery, the Maisondieu, the Blackfriars monastery, the cathedral," His eyes rested on the cruciform building, huge even from this distance, that sat like a mother hen among her chicks. Its three square towers made a shapely passion cross but were small in comparison with the central edifice whose lofty spire, this morning, was lost in a low ceiling of cloud.

McInnes surveyed the scene. Three separate attacks on the north and south gates and on the east or Pans Port would allow his caterans access to the church buildings at points farthest from the castle. There was no point in raiding through the town and arousing the castle guard. With luck, the cathedral would be well alight before the commander knew what was happening. He rode his horse at a walk outside the long south wall of the town, paying particular attention to its gates. Each was the same, a low arch in a thick wall, with a portcullis drop and a small guard-house. They could not be stormed, he thought, for, once alarmed, the iron portcullis would crash down and a very few defenders could stave off a hundred attackers. He rode on to the Pans Port. It was the farthest gate from the castle and nearest to the cathedral. This would have to be the one, he thought. As he passed, he counted four men-at-arms on the roadway on top of the wall. They wore antiquated iron helmets and breastplates that needed a good shine and held halberds across their shoulders. If they could be surprised, they could be cut down by two or three men. He positioned himself among the willows near the river and watched. He could not be seen and yet had a good view of the Pans Port, the gatehouse, and of the road that dipped through the river then meandered off towards the bishop's palace over the hill, to the harbour of Spynie and the salt-drying pans that gave the gate its name. Approaching the ford he saw three men leading two mules with baskets on their backs. He had an idea. He tied his horse to a tree, removed his jerkin, turned it inside out and put it on again, the tattered, dirty yellow fleece outside. He muddied his boots on the river-bank, tousled his hair and joined the muleteers as they arrived at the gate.

"Ho, there, open up for the bishop's fowlers," shouted one of them.

"Meal for the Maisondieu, ducklings for the rector and a fat drake for the man that winds the windlass!" called out another.

Two soldiers peered over the top of the gate and McInnes heard the click-clack of the windlass as the portcullis was slowly raised. The mules, the fowlers and Murdo McInnes passed through the Port and into the cathedral town of Elgin. Out of sight of the guard, Murdo gave a coin to each of the men. "Which alehouse do you frequent before you return home?" he asked. He was told and given directions to find it. Then he went with them to the Maisondieu where they delivered their meal-sacks.

When Murdo told his master he was going to reconnoitre the cathedral and the church buildings, Stewart had become thoughtful and charged him to seek out the young novice who had twice entered Lochindorb as the bishop's spokesman.

"Do not speak with him. Do not let him know who you are," the Wolf commanded. "Ask about him, what manner of fellow he is, and if he is man enough to draw sword against us as I believe him to be. Find out too if there are many like him among the monks and the novices. But it is he I want you to be able to recognise, when we return."

The Maisondieu was a group of low, connected buildings

94

surrounding the main hospital. This was a high-vaulted airy place which, nevertheless, stank of dirty, old and ill humanity. Inside, there were niches in the walls where men and women lay in all sorts of straits. At the far end was the food-board, loaded with bowls for porridge or broth, loaves of bread and a large pitcher of buttermilk. Lay brothers and monks moved among the residents, praying here, chastising there, renewing a straw mattress or emptying a piss-bucket. McInnes sat on a bench near the door among those who had come to seek help. He talked with his neighbours, a farmer and his wife who had taken their daughter there for absolution before she died. She was a shrivelled waif of eight who looked out at him through huge brooding eyes devoid of all expression save hopelessness. Her parents seemed quite resigned to the fact that the child had little time to live and told him she had been gored and trampled by a bull. She had recovered miraculously – good St Giles of the farmers had seen to that – but now her guts emptied on to her belly through the gore-hole and she was wasting away. She also smelt foully and they prayed she would be taken soon.

When his eyes grew accustomed to the gloom inside the hospital and his nose to the stink, Murdo studied the faces of the lay brothers as they worked. At Lochindorb, on the two occasions that the young man had appeared before them, he had been close enough for McInnes to remember – tall in stature, dark curly hair, pale face and solemn eyes. He spotted him almost at once and pointed him out to the farmer.

"Is that the brother you are waiting to see?" he asked.

"Mercy no! Thon's but a young novice. He canna shrive my bairn! A nice laddie for all that," he added, "the son of my superior at Duffus." He was evidently pleased to have this bit of information and sensing a willing listener he went on. "The man's deid noo – Hogeston of Plewlands. Got hisself killed twa year syne at Otterburn fighting the Percy. I was there myself – what a shambles!" He would have gladly talked at length on that subject but Murdo guided him back. "Aye, a dead man won that day. I've heard tell of that bloody business. But the young Hogeston, why is he here?"

"Och, he murdered a man and his father shipped him off to Paris, out of the way, I expect, and to study for the church. I dinna think he should have been so hard on his laddie. Though they could never prove it, we all ken it was a thief he killed with his long bow. Near Duffus, it happened," he said with some pride. "The laird's loon is no slouch wi a weapon. The arrow wis clean through the chest. I ken, for I had to bury the fellow. I'll wager ye, when the Wolf of Badenoch and his wild men go on the rampage, there will be others like Phil Hogeston wha'll gie the divil a fleg gin he tries tae dae a Forres on them!" He laughed at that and shortly after they had to take their wee lass to have her wound cleaned. "God! the jobs some folk have!" thought McInnes. He had heard enough and left the Maisondieu.

Before he rejoined the fowlers at their favourite howff he knew exactly how he would destroy the manses and the cathedral. But when he thought about the sick, the bairns and the old creatures, who lay helpless on their straw beds in the hospital, something in his war-hardened heart removed it from the buildings he had marked down for burning.

Twenty-four

A bright wood of birch-trees spread from the water's edge deep into the glen and between the silvered stems, hyacinths stood, like blue grass. A cuckoo sounded somewhere across the water and into that breath-holding silence rippled the music of woman-laughter.

"You are telling me that you are nineteen years old and have never known a man's love? I don't believe it. Goodness. When I was your age I had borne two sons and had known a dozen lovers! What is the matter with you? Is there none you fancy among the castle men? What about that big burly fellow called Walter? Him with the conceited hair-cut and the thick thighs?"

"Big Walt the slaughterer? No thank you! He smells of blood and finds his pleasures in Elgin. I could not look on a second-hand man! Besides, the girls giggle and say his face is the best part of him! No, my lady, I shall bide my time and, when the man I marry comes to me, I shall know him, never fear,"

"You are a strange girl, Hilda. With your auburn hair, your height and your cheeky freckled face, I would have expected you to have had a score of men by now. You must be telling me a story! Has no man lain with you? What about my own boys? Have they not had the good taste to woo you? Has Sandy never kissed you in the nursery!" Mariota laughed. Nursery days for Sandy and Hilda were long past.

"Have Walter or James shown no interest in what is under your blouse and beneath your skirt! Shame on them!" She cast a sideways glance at her maid and saw the flush spread on neck and cheeks.

"Aha! You blush! Come. Out with it. I will be surprised and disappointed if you have not caught the eye of at least one of my wild puppies! Was it Sandy?"

Hilda McDonnell's young body gave a small shiver. Mariota saw it.

"So, my beauty, you have been loved by my gallant Sandy! Still are, perhaps? And that is why you say you have no interest in boys – other boys. I can hardly blame you. My enigmatic James is as capable of knifing the one he loves as kissing her, but Sandy is the kindliest of my sons. Why look ashamed? He is a handsome boy, a little on the short side but his tight red curls and his blue eyes would win the heart of any woman. Have you known what it is like to lie with him? I wonder if you have! You are no prude. Is it a fear of getting with child that keeps you chaste? To bear a brat to a King's nephew is no great crime, better than to let some handsome dolt of a stableboy plant his miserable seed in you! Oh, I have been lucky, but I have also chosen well! Nothing less than a belted earl for me! By Sweet Jesus, if we take such a risk with our bodies why not make it worth the travail! At least, that is what I said to myself when I was your age. Now, it doesn't seem to matter so much, and a tall black-eyed curly-haired monk would suit me nicely! There has to be a challenge, you see, and to pit myself against the Holy church is a challenge. Truth to tell, I am getting a bit stale. Too much of the same thing is not good for a woman's pride. So I have set my heart on a monk, Hilda, and you are going to help me!"

"My lady," Hilda gave a surprised and frightened look, "what if your lord should get wind of it!"

"What if?" retorted Mariota. "I have made sure he gets wind of it, as you so picturesquely describe it! He is bent on this raid into Elgin. He is determined to blister the bishop's tonsured head and he is going to seize a certain monk so as to place our love on the gaming-table! He knows who has taken my fancy, et les jeux sont faites! You, my pretty young Hilda, you will be the decoy in this game of love. I shall draw you across my trail, I promise you, until both the Wolf and that splendid young monk are dizzy and quite confused. If I am going to have a love-affair now, it is going to be in the grand manner, reeking of passion, confused by lies, lingering, contrived and oh, so satisfying!"

Twenty-five

On the eve of the feast of St Botolph, anno domini thirteen hundred and ninety, the moon on its wane hung like a crusie-lamp above the forest of Badenoch. Tree shadows pointed stubby fingers at the loch and in that baleful half-light the castle lay like a toad on a lily leaf, the yellow spots of windows its small unblinking eyes. Then, it belched smoke and became a dragon.

In the forest, horses stamped on an aeon of blaeberry and pine-needles, men clanked in armour, called to each other through the trees and spurred their mounts to join the groups with which they would ride. Helmets nodded, scabbards slapped on leathern hose and the largest raiding party ever to leave Badenoch sallied forth from the lair of the Wolf.

On a hill high above the Abbey of Pluscarden and sweating in the warmth of the afternoon of the seventeenth of June, a dozen boys led some sixty horse in a wide circle, exercising them, waiting for the arrival of the tired steeds that would have carried the Earl of Buchan and his mounted men from Lochindorb to within sight of the spires of Elgin Cathedral.

From there on, the progress of the raiders was slow. They had ridden by firm tracks over dry moors. Now, in single file, they followed a burn that plunged through narrow defiles where men had to duck to avoid the lash of willow and birch, or meandered through marshy hollows, muddied by small black cattle, where clouds of hungry midges stung every inch of naked skin. To make matters worse, sixty cursing horsemen and a rabble of running men were held to a snail's pace by the carts, two creaking, jolting contraptions, each hauled unwillingly by its pair of mules. In the carts, wedged and fastened by ropes were barrels of wood-tar, kept soft, hot and reeking by the boys on the hill, braziers, fuel and stands of yard-long wooden staves, some feathered as arrows , each one with its point of tightly twisted heather-root. This was the weapon the Wolf had designed to scald the bishop's pate.

The bell of the monastery clanged its call to vespers. Half a mile away, their noise smothered by the trees, the invaders of that peaceful scene sweated and cursed their way out of the valley. When they forded the river Lossie two miles from the town, the sun had vanished behind the Hill of the Wangie and the cold thick mist from the sea blotted out the sky and chilled the air.

It was McInnes's plan to avoid the castle by riding in a wide half-circle round the town. Concealed by woods, the dusk and the haar, they reached the Pans Port without attracting any attention from the garrison. With his men around him, Alexander Stewart, Wolf of Badenoch, looked out from cover at his quarry. Rising like a wraith beyond the curve of the town-wall and made huge by the mist, the Gothic shape of the Cathedral of the Bishopric of Moray stood amidst its manses and their orchards.

"Right, McInnes, get us inside quickly," he commanded.

Two of the mules, now with small panniers slung across their rumps, each with a man atop and one in rear, picked their dainty-footed way through the thicket on the riverbank to the ford, out of sight in the fog both from the raiders and from the guard on the wall. From there, they approached the Pans Port.

"Ho there," shouted McInnes in rough imitation of the fowlers he had followed before. "Fat geese for the dean and a brace of mallard to open the gate."

The watchers heard the call and the clank of the windlass as it strained to lift its portcullis. The Wolf raised his arm, brought it sharply to his side and his men rushed out from the mist, to the open gate. The guards lay outside their little guardhouse, throats slit, their blood pulsing out on to the paved way that led to the manses. A tar-cart was hauled through the gate, the brazier set and lit and, as the barrel heated, the attack began. With shouts of battle the highlanders swooped on the homes of the clergy. Shrieks from the terrified families aroused everyone in the vicinity of the cathedral. Men and women ran for their lives in their night-dresses. A bell clanged a warning to the town as smoke began to rise slowly from the lath and thatch of the houses.

From the college grounds, and between the manses, a series of closes and enclosed passageways ran north to the Cathedral. Through those the raiders passed, laughing, confident in their unopposed strength. Suddenly they were halted. Four of the ten passages were blocked, each by a swordsman. To the whoops and shouts of the attackers was added the clash of steel and the shriek of wounding. McInnes understood at once what had happened and concentrated the wits of his men with a roar, "Through the farthest vennel and at them from the rear." Cutting, slashing, guarding, pushing, four young men left the mouths of their closes and retreated towards the doors of the church. One fell, stabbed by a cluster of hillmen, but yelled to his friend, "Leave me, Phil. I'll not die yet!" McInnes marked the man's companion. Yes, that was the monk who had come to Lochindorb, Philip Hogeston, fighting like a madman, but skilful and deadly. The door of the cathedral remained shut. The three swordsmen stood together and three gleaming arcs of steel cut and pierced the press of highlanders.

"Hold it!" The call came in Gaelic and the attackers stood back.

"Fight on, you cowards, or I'll cut you to pieces," shouted Hogeston. Swinging his sword like an axe, he rushed at his enemies. He heard rather than saw the net as it rustled above him, caught his sword point and entangled him in its knotted embrace. Men leapt at him and bound him tight. His weapon was wrenched from his grasp.

The closes were cleared and the tar-barrel, on its brazier and cart, was hauled nearer. Up went the flaming arrows, soaring in yellow sooty arcs to the roof and into the guttering of the great building, crashing through the windows to flame among the tapestries and woodwork inside. Sparks in clouds rose crackling from the chapter-house and from the manses. Despite McInnes's instructions, the hospital of the House of God, the Maisondieu, was destroyed by his wild men of Badenoch to whom nothing was sacrosanct. The night sky pressed down on a grisly scene, alight with the sulphur hue of hell.

Twenty-six

By midnight the cathedral was a crackling roaring furnace and its inhabitants were fleeing for their lives to the bishop's palace at Spynie three miles away. Bur himself had not shown face beyond its walls since the Sack of Forres. De Freskyn, the governor of the Castle of Elgin, now thoroughly alarmed by the blaze he could both see and smell, feared for the safety of the town and his military barracks at the foot of the castle hill. He sent a company of horsesoldiers clattering down the High Street to scout out the cause of the disturbance and of the burning. They returned at the gallop to tell him that the Wolf of Badenoch and a thousand wild highlandmen, mounted and on foot, controlled the north and the south ports and were driving the townspeople like cattle towards the castle. De Freskyn's action was to slam the castle gates, bar them fast and man the battlements, a desperate overreaction that allowed the invaders a free hand and afforded the governor only a view of a burning town.

When the magnificent Gothic building resembled a huge funeral pyre, the enthusiasm of the attackers waned. Revenge was complete and the Wolf turned his small army to the road home. The church of St Giles and houses between the burning cathedral and the castle were given the same treatment, "To use up the hot pitch," as McInnes said. Then, for good measure they set fire to the Abbey of Pluscarden and its red glow lit their way through the glens as far as the forest of Darnaway.

Hogeston lay on his stomach across the back of a hill-pony, secured like a gralloched stag. Many hours later the Wolf and his marauders reached Lochindorb and, still in the net, the novice was lowered into its dungeon to await the pleasure of his captor. There he remained in darkness for two days.

"I have a prisoner to show you," the Wolf said to Mariota. "He is that monk who had the audacity to serve me the Papal Bull of Excommunication." He watched Mariota's face but saw in it no sign of anything more than a faint interest. "I have never found the man I cannot break," he continued, "and this young pup will be no exception. When I have finished with him I shall give you the pleasure of disposing of the rubbish!"

From the castle dungeon where escape was impossible, the monk was taken to the Wolf. Although his body was weakened by fatigue and thirst, his spirit showed no signs of flagging. He stood in front of his tormentor and taunted him. "Does your left shoulder still pain you, my Earl Buchan? If my aim had been true four years ago I would not be here! Nor you either!"

Alexander Stewart glowered at the man who stood a spitting distance from him. The fellow had taken him by surprise. "By Christ," he said softly but with sudden conviction, "You must be the young pup that winged me that night in midsummer at the Long Steps!"

"I should have killed you," said Hogeston, "for you had killed my friend less than an hour before, on the shore at the Bay of the Primroses. And what of the bishop's gold, the candlesticks and the chalices? How many murders did you pay off with them – or have you fashioned your drinking vessels from them, or ornaments for your whore?" The Wolf leapt on him and struck him across his face. Blood flowed from a gashed lip. "Unmanacle me, Stewart, and try that again," snarled the prisoner.

"Hawk, take this vindictive viper to the water-pit. Unmanacle him as he desires. Chains rust in water and iron makes poor food for fish!"

The water-pit was a hole hewn in the rock on which the castle was built and was connected to the water outside by crevices and fissures. At the height of summer when the level of the loch was low, a man could stand mid-thigh in water. Into this wet man-hole Philip Hogeston was thrown and a wooden lid pushed over the top to shut out the light of day. No prisoner had ever escaped this noisome pit, but Hogeston, spurred on by rage as much as by fear, succeeded. Murder was in his heart, as like the mythical water-kelpie he crept, dripping, up the corridors and stairs of the castle searching for one man, the Wolf of Badenoch. He very nearly succeeded. Only acrobatic dexterity and the speed of the Hawk's foot saved his master's life.

Following that assault, the Wolf spoke again with Mariota. "We have a wildcat in our castle," he said. "The prisoner I took at the sack of Elgin Cathedral came near to murdering me a second time." He described how the avenger from the water-pit had seized him by the throat, and described to her in detail for the first time the ambush at the Long Steps across the eastern narrows of the Loch of Spynie where he had been wounded four years before.

"I admire persistence and bravery in any man and, for the present, I have decided to spare his life. If I cannot subdue his spirit by physical means I can perhaps sap it in some other way. I have it in mind to make this warrior monk my personal priest, and pit his belief against my heresies. Ha! I shall enjoy acting as 'The Devil on the mountain top' – 'all these things will I give thee if thou wilt fall down and worship me'! We shall soon see whether the power of his godliness matches the power in his arm! And, when I tire of my game of cat and mouse, you, my beauty, shall tell me how I shall get rid of him." He was watching Mariota closely as he spoke but saw nothing to fire his jealousy. "I have locked him in the Jesus tower. He will feel like a caged animal but, if he truly has the makings of a priest as well as of a warrior, my wooden Christ will cool his passion."

Mariota smiled to herself. "So this," she thought, "is why he took my beautiful statue from Loch-an-Eilean and set it up in his tower-room. He planned to capture this man. Is it possible that my brash and wilful lord is possessed of a subtilty and a perception I have so far failed to notice?" Then for the first time in months she offered her mouth to him and submitted to his embrace with an eagerness she had long withheld.

Twenty-seven

The Wolf's captive did not surprise him. For a night and two days, his shouts and blasphemies could be heard across the loch, but by the second evening there was a silence in the west tower. When dawn broke on the third day the prisoner awoke and saw, neatly piled inside the door, his boots, breeches, his linen, his jerkin and, his heart leaped, his sword, dagger and shield. He tried the handle of the door. It swung open and stone steps wound out of sight towards the courtyard. He sat on his mattress of straw and pondered this sudden and unexpected change in his fortune. Why? Had he a friend in this wild place who would risk his life to set him free? More likely, he thought, this is a trap, a simple trick set by the Wolf.

He dressed, unsheathed his sword and slowly, silently, on bare feet, descended the stair. It was dark in the narrow space between the outer wall and the keep, but a glimmer of light through the watergate showed that the portcullis was raised. A small boat bobbed quietly on the lap of the loch, tempting, tempting. Quickly he turned and climbed back to his cell. He was no fool. There would be another occasion, less fortuitously presented perhaps, but of his own choosing, when he could escape. Some other chance would come; by some other way he would leave this fortress, when it was expedient for him to do so.

"I'm glad he didn't grasp the chance to escape. Hawk, why do you think he threw it away?" Mariota reined her horse on the summit of the hill and gazed at her castle on its loch in the broad miles of moorland that rolled west and north to the forest of the Findhorn.

"Because he is not an idiot, my lady. Because your plan smelled to him of a trap, as I told you it would. I watched him glide from the tower to the centre of the court. I could feel him thinking. 'It is too easy. If I take that small boat beyond the battlements I will hear the twang of a bow, the zip of an arrow, nothing more.' Then he did a strange thing. He stood quite motionless as if waiting for some sign. An Oyster-catcher fluttered black and white across the water. Quickly he hurled his dagger, the fancy one I showed you with the naked lady carved on its hilt, far out into the loch, sighed and returned quietly to his cell. Here he will stay. He will accept the challenge my lord will make when he offers him the position of priest to the Wolf of Badenoch. In time I will have the story of that slim, wicked dagger, how he came by it and why he flung it away. He is an interesting fellow and I shall enjoy unbending him."

Mariota de Athyn smiled. Despite what the Hawk thought, every piece of her plan had fallen into place. The handsome monk was caught in her web, which the Wolf fondly fancied was of his own spinning. Men, how simple they were! It was now time to draw a false scent across the trail and, to do this, she relied on the undoubted beauty of Hilda MacDonnell and the challlenge of her chastity.

Twenty-eight

"Hilda, you are either the greatest prude that ever lived or a very accomplished liar! I know that something out of the ordinary happened while we were at Balvenie Castle and that it took place when you and Hogeston went back the way we had come and searched for my serpent." Mariota picked the twisted band of gold off her bedroom table. The emerald eyes of the wildcats in its clasp shone wickedly.

"Yes, I know that you and he found my lovely chain and I am glad, but you returned to Balvenie alone and with a gleam in your eye that certainly was not there when you left me. You told me that Philip Hogeston had decided to go back to Lochindorb. He gave no reason you say, but there was reason enough the day after, on his bruised and bloodied face. Come now, Hilda, virgin though you claim you still are, I doubt even your nails could have marked that man so, and left his face, even seven days later, like a piece of butcher-meat. I want the truth from you."

Hilda McDonnell hung her head. "We rode out from Balvenie and had gone only four miles up the burn-side when I spied a golden gleam among the dead leaves in the water. I was overjoyed to have found it. Hogeston dismounted too and before I could guess his intention he had me on my back among the blaeberries." Hilda raised her head and saw the look on her mistress's face and blushed. "Nothing happened, my lady. I struggled free when McInnes arrived, and left the men snarling at each other like two wolves."

"And if Murdo McInnes had not arrived so fortuitously?" Mariota hung her question in the air. The colour faded from Hilda's cheek. "He would have done what he wished to do. I could not have fought him for ever."

"And would you have struggled for long, my little Hilda?"

A blush stole again into the girl's cheek. In a small voice she whispered, "I shall never know the answer, my lady. He is a handsome brute as well as a powerful one."

Mariota laughed and gathered the slim young figure into her arms. "You are learning, ma petite. Sometimes it is necessary to fight, but it is prudent, less dangerous, and certainly more pleasant, not to fight for too long! But there are other ways of overcoming a man. Do you not love this Hogeston just a little?" Hilda shook her head quickly.

"Even if he was not beyond my station in life I would not love him."

Mariota sat before her shining silver mirror.

"Brush my hair, Hilda," she commanded gently.

As her long wheaten tresses cascaded over her shoulders she said, "It is time I taught this arrogant priest a lesson. I doubt he knows aught beyond the tricks of the whorehouses, and to force a woman is no way to her heart. Let us make a plan, you and I! Always, ma cherie, there must be a plan. My life, to you, may seem to move on its course with little spurring from me. That is not so. A woman's destiny is in her own hands. She must set her heart on what she wants from life then, like puppets dangling on strings from her fingers, she must move these thickheads of men with their codes of justice, or chivalry, or ambition, in the direction she wants them to move. Else, what a dull life we should lead, you and I! Consider now, Philip Hogeston. I do not for a moment believe his presence here as prisoner or priest is by accident. Not so. My vain lord has judged aright my interest in this courageous monk and, because my lord loves me, he is jealous. Learn now, my innocent Hilda, that a jealous man is soft clay in a woman's hand! If I want to make him a little more jealous, would he not love me more! If he expects me to make doe's eyes at his priest he will not be disappointed!"

Hilda's eyes grew larger as her mistress spoke.

"My lady, you take a risk when you seek to inflame my lord's passion. He is a just man, but not a kind one. I have seen him thrash his sons for their small misdeeds. To make cuckold of him would drive him mad. Hogeston would hang, and you, my lady, what might become of you!"

Hilda's hands hung limp at her side. The brushing had stopped. Mariota turned and looked at her. Hilda had never seen her like this before, excited, triumphant.

"Do you not understand at all what spurs a man to deeds and what determines the way he acts? You are right. My lord would go mad! During all the years I have lived with him he has made certain that any intrigue which might violate his possessions was snapped at its root. Do you remember what happened to the young English knight, Edward de Sandbach, who was foolish enough to forget himself when I danced for them. He touched me! And instantly the earl in a rage rose from the table and pulled him by his long curled hair from the hall! I swear he would have killed him had the boy's father not quickly intervened. He soothed the earl's ruffled feathers by scolding his son – 'he had too much to drink, my lord' – and gifted the earl on the spot a piece of his Cheshire estate!

"Andrew will inherit Sandbach when he comes of age, so my dancing that night was worth something!

"Yes, we play with fire when we play on men's passions. But their vanity overrides them all! For my lord to be made a cuckold would be bad enough – but to admit it, never! He is to be gone soon, before the snow drifts high at Drumochter pass, to complete the bargain for young James' betrothal to Janet Menzies of Strath Tay. He will have the Appin of Dull as part of her dowry. He needs it to strengthen his grip on his southern lands and he intends to start building a castle at Garth for James and his bride. He will be away from home for longer than ever before. If I do not have Philip Hogeston knocking on my door in the first week of his absence, I am not the woman I thought myself to be!"

Twenty-nine

Snow sat heavily on the forest and carpeted the ice on Lochindorb. A full moon rolled across the sky, plucked tiny sparks from the frosted loch and painted the icy mountains in steely grey. The fortress cast a black and jagged shadow and smoke from its lums drifted in pale wreaths slowly towards the frozen shore. Inside the castle, doors were shut against the cold and men and women huddled close to roaring fires.

For hours two men had gamed in silence and the opposing armies of chessmen, armed knights on their painted palfreys, rooks, queens, kings and simple labouring pawns, delicate but unadorned, were gradually thinned out into a tight strategic design. Philip Hogeston's left hand caressed a captive queen, fingering her bare little breasts and tiny ivory feet. He stole a glance at the woman by the fire. She sat in a cushioned inglenook. Her arms peeped from long purple half-sleeves and her busy hands worked a tapestry. Purple was her colour, he mused. It complimented the pale coils of her silky hair and the pallor of her breasts. Her face, shaped like a lover's heart carved on a tree, lifted and their eyes met. In that moment he knew for certain that her thoughts were not all on the pattern before her, but, like his own, had leaped ahead into the night. He felt his eyebrows tingle.

"Checkmate!" Alexander's hard voice cut through his dreaming. "You make it easy for me, priest, when your concentration is loose. Why is it that you play so much better against the earl? Do you think I am a less worthy opponent? I shall lead armies and shall capture real kings and queens before I am old. James, fill my cup. I find this fellow tedious and his game poor!"

Alexander stretched his arms above his curly head and yawned. "You will have to play and not dream, Hog, to remain in the earl's favour. Mother, I'll say goodnight. James, we have much to do tomorrow and Father will not forgive us if we lie abed when we should be up and mounted. We meet him, remember, at the Bridge of Carr at sun-up." Philip rose from his seat and the brothers saluted their mother; he bowed towards Mariota. Again, those soft eyes and the enigmatic raising of the eyebrows. He felt young James's keen look on him, and his hostility.

"Good-night, young lords," Mariota said. "Good-night, Master Hogeston, and pleasant dreams."

Was that high, bell-like, womanly voice devoid of feeling? Alexander and James left the room. He stopped beside her to take a light from the fire.

"Surely you know your way around the castle without the need of a taper!" He looked at her but she had returned her eyes to her coloured threads. Then, softer than a breath of summer wind, "Au revoir," she said.

The darkness in the long panelled corridor was lit by four wall lamps. Like yellow stars, they failed to dispel the night but rather altered its texture and its intensity to a transparent sepia. Even without the glimmer from these small pools of tallow he would have found his way down the stairs, round the sharp corners, along narrow low-ceilinged corridors to the courtyard and to his cell in the northwest tower. Now, as he left the room and closed the door behind him, he was gripped by a wild excitement. His thoughts somersaulted to his first week of captivity in Lochindorb. Then, after days and nights of fear, torment, rage and self-pity, the bolts of his prison had been mysteriously drawn and freedom had beckoned to him from a little bobbing boat on the dawn-lit loch. Why had he not rowed away from the gaunt fortress when the chance lay so temptingly before him? Was it, as he had nearly persuaded himself, that his curiosity demanded he should stay to find out more about his villainous captor? In that moment as he stood outside her room, he knew that even then he had lusted for white breasts, long silken hair, and for smooth thighs he had not even seen.

At the Maisondieu, where he had spent his novice year after knowing the flesh-pots of Paris, his imagination had fed on the tales that were told in the dormitory, of the beauty of the mistress of the Wolf of Badenoch, of her sensuality. Whispered at night when they lay on their mattresses, or laughed about in the alehouses of Elgin, many and lewd were the stories that had collected around this woman, Mariota de Athyn. The Wolf's bawd, the justiciar's Jezebel, they called her. How different was the reality! When he first set eyes on her at the long high table in Lochindorb where she sat beside the raven-haired earl, she was nearly thirty, but her years only added to her beauty. Experience had brought her poise, engendered by an awareness of the emotions she aroused, and a remarkable dignity that held men in thrall. During the months he had spent in Lochindorb Castle, he had first regarded her, he thought, like a priest, with interest but as his moral inferior. Then the aura of her complete womanhood, the way she walked, and sat, and listened and laughed, quickly penetrated the thin, protective, priestly shell. Finally, desire flamed within him, fed by the most subtle of invitations – a look, a raising of an eyebrow, the turn of her head, a mocking laugh, especially when she demonstrated her clear superiority on horseback. So was his manhood pricked, humbled, occasionally flattered, and always he was drawn to her, as iron is to a lodestone, as dust to amber.

But nothing she had said to him, no look she had ever given, was so explicit in its invitations as those she had quietly passed to him that evening. Philip Hogeston knew that if he did not pursue his desire now it was unlikely that he would get another chance. There would be an end to whatever might be between him and Mariota. He would be shamed in his own estimation as well as in hers, as a faint heart and a coward.

When he reached the courtyard he snuffed the flame of his taper and quickly and stealthily returned to her chamber. He knew he had closed her door as he left. It was now ajar. With sudden certainty, he pulled his black cowl over his head and slipped inside. There was an arras to kill the draughts and he crouched behind it and held his breath.

Hilda McDonnell knelt by the fire prodding the glowing peats, her hearing dulled, he hoped, by the hiss and crack of the flames. She gave no sign that she had heard or sensed his entrance. The chamber was small, dimly lit, but the slightest movement of his cloak could give him away.

For a moment he regretted his audacity. Although the Wolf was away, there were many in the castle who would be quick to report on the unusual sight of the priest tip-toeing along the corridors towards or from Mariota's room at dead of night. He was set now on a dangerous course that, as for other enemies of Alexander Stewart Lord of Badenoch, might end as a cold, bloated corpse in the water-pit. Had he misjudged the signals he thought Mariota had sent him tonight? If so, this adventure could finish for him on the point of a dagger. Neither James nor Alexander would hesitate. For James it would be a pleasure!

He crouched, motionless, behind the thin screen, sweat on his palms, his mouth dry, and felt rather than heard the door close behind him. Nothing happened and then Mariota joined her maid by the fire. She stood before her tall silver mirror, between the firelight and his gaze, and through the silken nightdress he saw the faint blur of her nakedness. She turned, sat on a stool and warmed herself in the fire's glow. "Hilda, come and do my hair." Hilda McDonnell unfastened the long rich tresses that were plaited round her face, then with slow strokes of a brush she straightened and softened them until the hair curled like a pale wave around her hips.

After a while Mariota said, "That will do. Good-night Hilda." Did her voice sound a little strained, her words stilted? The maid tidied the dresser, put away the brushes, curtsied and replied, "Good-night my lady."

Philip heard the clip-clop of sandalled feet across the room. There was a small creak as the door opened, a tiny gust of cold air, and silence. Philip waited. Mariota's voice, like a muted bell, floated across the room:

"Come to the fire, Master Hogeston."

The blood rushed to his face and he obeyed. He stood before her, tall, cloaked, his unruly hair struggling out beneath the cowl, just as she remembered it.

"In loving, if not in living, there must be equality." She loosened the tie at her throat and the dark silk slid down over her shoulders, breasts, hips.

"Take off your clothes," she commanded.

Philip Hogeston stood, bemused. This was not at all as he had imagined it would be, but when his eyes devoured the soft, lovely, shapely woman who sat before him he did as she told him.

"Yes, Philip," she said quietly, as if reading his thoughts. "You so nearly fled away through that door. If you had done so, you would never know what you had missed and there would never have been another invitation. But you could not leave me now. You will stay and we shall be lovers. And when cock-crow comes you will have been bewitched, and you will have been my slave." He hesitated no more. On his knees before her, he lifted her hands from her lap and pressed them to his lips, then with a sigh sank his face against her breasts.

Indeed he was bewitched by that princess of love, that queen of seduction, and during the swift hours, in the misty glow of the peat-fire, he saw the naked lust of Aphrodite and felt the high sharp shock of fulfilled desire.

When he lay in his own bed high above the silent loch and watched the soft fingers of dawn steal into his room, he raised his arms again as if to pull her towards him, and once more, in a purple dream, he saw the swinging breasts, felt soft thighs against his flanks and the rhythmic rise and fall of hips as they soared together, above mortal lust, to godlike ecstasy.

Thirty

A month after he arrived home from Garth in the Appin of Dull, Alexander Stewart summoned his acquaintances and his neighbours to a feast at Lochindorb Castle. It required no imagination and little intelligence to know that by then a deep and dangerous chasm lay between Mariota and the Wolf of Badenoch. This had been plain ever since he had ridden home, amid a flurry of late snow, in the company of his two sons Alexander and James. Probably because she felt the weight of her guilt so heavy on her, Hilda McDonnell was immediately aware of the change and realised that it meant only one thing. Somehow the Wolf knew that the bait he had been at such pains to dangle before Mariota had been taken, that the young novice with the careless mop of hair and the bold eyes had made him a cuckold under his own roof. Daily, his rage mounted and still he did nothing.

Then came the feast. For all present it was a nightmare. For the guests, the ordeal began from the moment they disembarked at the watergate. Yet everything had been prepared for their comfort. Nothing had been overlooked. It was May and the snows of a long winter lingered in the corries. The rivers ran high and salmon were plentiful. Grilled, baked, boiled, smoked, their delectable pink flesh adorned the table. Early lambs too, born in the ice of February and grown to plumpness on spring pastures, provided the meat for a board that groaned under its weight of food. The last of the French claret was served. This was the Wolf's share of wine gifted to the Scottish royals by Admiral Jean de Vienne, who commanded fifty French knights and their thousand men-at-arms seven years before when they had come to encourage "les pauvres Ecossais" in their struggle against Richard of England. Barrels of that fine wine were broached and it was served in golden goblets. But gloom persisted and not even the capering Hawk could lift it. His humour was quick and acid, but no one had the courage to applaud his jokes. The Wolf sat, aloof in his large chair. He ate little, drank a lot and brooded, like some huge raven, over an assembly which was unnaturally hushed.

Later she knew, but hovering in the background between the nursery and the hall, carrying little plates of meat and sweetmeats to her young charges, Margaret and Andrew, Hilda McDonnell wondered if, perhaps, it was the brilliant devoted dwarf who, in a moment of despair over jealousy, had informed on his mistress. Or had James, the tortuous, black-hearted James, poisoned his father's thoughts with suspicions, based on what he deduced, or even on what he knew? As she watched the fearful drama unfold, as she saw her beautiful mistress sit, tense and white-faced, the notion came to her that Mariota herself, made reckless by the bravado of conquest, could have been the one to unleash the deadly secret, to taunt the earl with her infidelity!

Suddenly Alexander Stewart sent the long table crashing and the platters and jugs rolling on the floor. In a voice that shook the rafters he shouted:

"'Priest, damned priest, perfidious priest, and you woman, why have you destroyed me? What have you done to me? Know ye, my friends, that these two," – he pointed his accusing finger first at Hogeston and then at Mariota – "that these two are in secret league with the Devil and that witchery and foul magic pervade this place!"

He poured forth a list of signs, portents and occasions which, he swore, now convinced him of their sorcery. There was the mystery of the disappearance of McInnes's horse, which broke its tether, left its locked stable and was never seen again. There were the methods used by Hogeston to cure the child Andrew of the croup when the boy lay at death's door. According to Stewart, "they were naught but sorcery of Baal."

On the eve of Christmas, six fat geese with their necks pulled had flapped their way from the kitchens, padded silently into the hall with their heads trailing behind them and performed a grotesque dance of death before the lord's table.

Whatever the truth of these allegations, the effect was catastrophic. The earl's two oldest sons leapt forward. Alexander, a knife in his fist, challenged his father to withdraw his accusation against his mother. The other James, spat in Hogeston's face, screamed curses at him and swore that he, James Stewart, would send him to Hell!

Next day Hogeston himself provided the proof of his witchcraft by vanishing from the castle. The Wolf had set a guard on his actions, yet no one saw him go.

Mariota, accompanied by Hilda McDonnell, the baby Margaret and the faithful Hawk, were escorted on their long journey into Buchan, and banishment. Even in the loneliness of King Edward Castle, they were not for long left in peace. Alexander Stewart, determined to hurt her, arranged marriage between the child Margaret and Robert, heir to the Earldom of Sutherland, and took the young girl forcibly from her mother.

"Later, my lady was reunited with her youngest, and lives in contentment with her at Dornoch Castle."

Thirty-one

On that statement by Hilda McDonnell, John Hamilton's manuscript finished. The tale petered out in a most disappointing way. Surely, I thought, Mariota, the quixotic Mariota, could not have ended her days amid the dull domestic bliss of Dornoch Castle. History records that Robert, Earl of Sutherland, and Margaret, sole daughter of the Wolf of Badenoch, begot a large family. I could not imagine Mariota as the dutiful granny.

There were other leads to the story that I had already followed up. I knew for example that Philip Hogeston had not used sorcerer's magic to vanish out of Lochindorb. He had escaped and, to avoid the wrath of The Wolf, and of the Church, had joined the chivalric order of St John of Jerusalem, as a combatant, and fought in the Sixth Crusade. Later he had reappeared at his family's estate in Moray, married to a French nobleman's daughter, Bridget de Dreux. I knew too that Bridget had visited Mariota at Dornoch Castle, in search of the truth of her husband's incarceration at Lochindorb.

I felt absolutely certain there was more yet to know and that the bishop's tale did not end as it seemed to, with a question-mark. If I had learned one thing about Bishop John Winchester it was that he had an insatiable curiosity which compelled him to go on asking questions, sieving out the truth until he knew, or thought that he knew, all.

Suddenly, like a blow, it hit me that there would be no point in concealing a confession in a lead box, and burying it under a flag-stone in his fortress at Spynie, if the bishop had not finally unravelled the truth. And it had to be an unpalatable truth that he had hidden so securely within his palace walls.

John Hamilton, curator of the Museum of Antiquities where "The Winchester Papers" are a prized possession, in his first assault on that treasure of scroll and parchment, had come upon a conundrum. Written in the square hand of Bishop John was what he and I referred to as "The Bishop's Riddle". It ended:

"Wha slew the Wolf and his whelp of Garth
Adultery, witchcraft, or God's Own Wrath?" That was what Bishop Winchester had wanted to know; not, literally, how the Wolf had died. That knowledge, however interesting to us, was of less importance to a man of God in the fifteenth century than what, or who, had slain the Devil in his soul! Had it been Bishop Bur, as the Church firmly believed then, and ever since? Had it been a woman, Mariota de Athyn? Or had it been neither! What had persuaded the Wolf to go on his knees at a Ceremnony of Humiliation in Perth Cathedral to the man he detested enough to try and destroy? What had persuaded him to part with a huge slice of his fortune in reparation for the fiery fury of his vandalism, for the destruction of two towns, an abbey and a great cathedral? Was it God, or Mammon? The bishop was no one's fool. Although he believed in the power of the Almighty he had to know the truth. And so had I.

I picked up the phone and dialled John Hamilton's number. As I heard it ringing in his house, I noticed the hour – three AM.! I let it ring. It rang for a long time. When at last he answered I spared him banal apologies.

I asked him, "Are you concealing any part of Hilda McDonnell's testament from me, John Hamilton?"

There was a silence at the other end of the line, so long that, had I not heard him breathing, I would have thought the connection had gone dead.

"You wake me up at this hour of night to ask me that! You must be daft! The answer I give you, if only to get you off my back, and allow me some sleep, is 'Yes,' and you can bloody well come and decipher the bishop's script yourself!"

He hung up and I was left with the maddening urge to cross the Grampians once more, and instantly.

Thirty-two

There was more, much more. Bishop Winchester had learned truths which shocked him. About the time these events occurred, one John Resby, a follower of John Wykcliffe, was lashed to a stake at Perth and burned alive. He was the first of the reforming martyrs and died for pointing a finger at corruption in the Church. Because of what the bishop was told by Hilda McDonnell, her testimony lay hidden for five hundred years! Separately wrapped, and written down at a later date, came this epilogue, or codicil, to her covenant with John Winchester. "I learned of the death of the Wolf of Badenoch from the oldest of his family, Sir Alexander, the Earl of Mar since his rough wooing of the widowed countess. He came to the croft of Auchtertipper in the spring, parted with his horsemen at the pass and rode across the burn, under the soft pink gean trees, to our cottage. Through the door, I watched him come. He shouted, 'Murdo McInnes, I have news for you.'

"Murdo was in the kail patch and I was showing Jenny, our seven year old, how to bake bannocks. Murdo had not met Lord Sandy since he had discharged his bond to him after the audacious raid on Kildrummy Castle to capture the countess. Lord Sandy had thought it better to sink out of sight following that episode, for however profitable he reckoned his marriage to the Countess of Mar, he knew he had made powerful enemies. So he went a-pirating the English sea trade and offered to take McInnes with him, but Murdo took his discharge from his service. He had no stomach for piracy, however lucrative, even with such a captain!

"Murdo walked up the hill to where his master sat astride his horse, stiff and straight in the saddle. Lord Sandy greeted his father's henchmen. 'The Wolf is dead,' he said. Murdo admitted to me afterwards that although he was scarcely surprised, it was as if a piece of him had been sliced off. Lord Sandy must have seen the effect that his words had on him. He dismounted and took McInnes by the arm. "Steady old man,' he said kindly. 'No one is immortal.' He continued. 'The Wolf died in Castle Garth and during his last months he was cared for by my brother James. He died a diseased and shrunken shadow of the Wolf who pillaged Elgin. James did all that he could for him.'

"To gather his wits and to conceal his emotion, Murdo asked what brought the lord Alexander to Badenoch, since Lochindorb no longer belonged to his family.

"'I came to see you Murdo,' Sandy replied, 'and also to see what the vandals have done to my old home.'

"'Ach, the Comyns pulled it to bits, when the word came from Edinburgh,' said Murdo. 'It was as if they wanted to tear the heart from the old Justiciar. It will sadden you to see Lochindorb now.'

"Alexander's face went grim. 'The foxes take a lot on themselves when they sink their teeth in a dying Wolf and the score will be settled some day!'

"The Earl of Mar looked carefully at my husband. 'You won a good woman when you married Hilda McDonnell. Did you ever meet again he whom my father called The Hog?' There was a faint wrinkling round his eyes for a moment. Then the grim look returned. 'By Sweet Jesus, that ill-made monk has much to answer for to James! My brother daily feeds his hate and craves for the moment their paths will cross. For myself, I cannot blame Philip Hogeston for all the misery that descended upon my father. I was never a party to his vindictive attacks on the Holy Church, as you know, and believe in my innermost heart he has suffered the wrath of God's outrage!'

"By that time, I ventured to approach the two men. Lord Alexander looked at me in that way I knew of old, a mix of hauteur and noblesse oblige. I challenged his stare, and was rewarded by the smallest of smiles, which I returned. It was as if he briefly acknowledged the years we shared as children; and our intimacies at sixteen.

"'Can you tell me aught about my Lady Mariota de Athyn?' I asked him. The warmth, little that there was of it, left his face.

"'My sister Margaret accepted her mother to her household at Dornoch, against my advice. With her preoccupation for collecting holy relics and her enthusiasm for an ever changing train of religious charlatans, she has brought on herself the distress of her daughter and the derision of her daughter's folk. She is a mad woman, lost in a world peopled by devils and saints.'

"It was scarcely two years after our meeting with Lord Sandy, that I received a mysterious message from Lady Mariota. I cannot forget the occasion, for it came within a month of the death of our only child Jenny.

"A short time after Murdo returned from his pilgrimage to Lochindorb Castle with the Earl of Mar, he began to cough. They had spent a night together among its ruins, and the evil vapours in that place afflicted him. He lay ill for most of the summer. I did the herding for him, with Jenny's help. It was a cold wet year and our oat crop failed. Winter came with snow, ice, and no feed for the hens and little for us. I never want to live again through such a winter. Yet by some miracle, in the following spring my husband was well enough for the sowing. Then Jenny became ill. She lay that long year in her cot, her eyes growing larger, her body thinner, her cough harsher. Yet her cheeks were red as the rowan berries. She lay in the darkness of the croft and listened to the curlew on the hill, the scraiking of the plovers and the whirr of the snipe. She could hear them when they were beyond our earshot. When May came, she died. Her last words were, 'Hark to the cuckoo in the gean blossom!' The cuckoo's first song brings a sob to my heart even now. Poor Jenny.

"That very month, a stranger appeared at our door. He was an 'Egyptian', a small tough tinker-man with curly black hair, high cheeks, and a swarthy face. He was dressed in a patchwork of old skins and spoke only in the Gaelic.

"'Greetings, Hilda McDonnell. The night of your sorrow has

123

almost passed. Do not grieve for your child for she is with the Blessed Virgin in Heaven. The Holy Ghost, the God of Jacob, hath punished, and now He forgives. I bring you greeting from your mistress, Mariota. These are her words, not mine. She begs you to come to her, and to tell you that, for her, the wrath of God is nigh. She would be shriven if she could be believed!'

"Not for a moment did I question one word he told me. My lady had known of Jenny's death without ever being told she had been born! That miracle was enough to tell me that Mariota needed me and, when I repeated the man's story to Murdo, he said simply, 'We must go with him.'

"I asked the stranger how far he had come and where my lady Mariota lived now.

"He replied, 'A league or two this side of Ultima Thule!'

"We loaded what we could on to two horses and, when we left, we had stripped our croft of Auchtertipper bare. Our companion was a cheery fellow, full of old tales and songs, and our weeks together passed easily. He was born, so he told us, in Hibernia, and, like all whom we have met from that place, he claimed descent in the royal line from the High King Brian Buroo. If we had believed he spoke the truth only half of the time he opened his mouth, we would have believed too much!

"After many days he led us to a place where the mountains met the western ocean and salt-water lapped quietly on a seaweed shore. Little boats, too frail to manage the waves and the winds of the open sea, bobbed and curtseyed on a mirror of forest and snow. Mac Eth, as our guide called himself, pointed to a goat-track that zigzagged from our feet to the skyline, between mountain heads that bowed to each other under the blue canopy of heaven. 'There is our path, and as steep beyond, but down, to hallowed land.' Even our horses took fright at such a fearsome ascent, laying their ears flat and tossing their manes in disbelief. I dared not look back. Then we were at the summit, and there were the wild hills beyond Glen Torridon, that humped and slid their massive bulk out of a blue–green ocean."

Thirty-three

So they came to the place that Mac Eth called Applecross, to the cell of Gillanders the Culdee and to the abode of Mariota. The evening sun threw a long narrow shadow from Raasay across the inner sound and touched the sandy bay with silver. Far beyond were the chopped-off hills of the Quiraing. From the heights above the village, across a sea that flashed like the scales on a giant mackerel, they had seen a whale-like shape which was the island of Harris. Mac Eth had not exaggerated when he told them, back in Badenoch, that they would travel to within a league or two of Ultime Thule!

They rode their horses down to the beach, passed a scattered village of black houses and in the shallows, the wide circle of its salmon-trap. The animals joyfully splashed ankle-deep in the cool clear sea. Ahead, the mouth of a valley opened; a burn flashed free between faded alders and the ox-blood brilliance of wild cherry, and smoke rose behind a stand of yellow oaks.

Mac Eth watered the horses in a pool above the sea-wrack and led the way into the glade. Murdo and Hilda looked at each other in astonishment. It was as if their load of fatigue, doubt and anxiety slipped from them on to the machair. They rounded a bend. There, in its little glen, stood a church. It was small, built of slates and turfed with slabs of peat. A celtic cross, a slender monolith, pointed to heaven and, around its base, the tangle of a thorn-tree dripped its red rose-hips like the blood of our Lord!

There was a stable nearby and hens clucking about an empty grain-basket. Beyond, two small cots sat side by side, smaller than the church, built from the same black stone and thatched with river-rush. Farther away, on what seemed the verge of this holy ground, was a long low building, turfed, walled in the manner of the houses in the village from rounded sea-pebbles set in clay. Smoke rose from the roof-hole and hung like a blue scarf over the valley.

Mac Eth gave a whistle and a hound appeared in the door of one of the cottages, its head aslant and as big as a dog seal's, its coat shaggy like a mountain ram's. It moved not a muscle, but stood, ears pricked, looking directly at us. Then it gave a yowl of recognition and bounded toward its master.

"Lulach, my beauty." Mac Eth laughed, staggering under the weight of affection, a large pink tongue devouring his face. "Down fellow; down. Mariota's deer-hound," he explained, "But mine on the mountain."

Someone else stood in the low door of the croft, regarding them fixedly. From where they stood, Murdo and Hilda could not decide if it was a man or woman. Above a sable coat that reached the ground, a white face was framed in a cap of grey untidy hair that fell in wisps and tow-ends over the collar. Mac Eth stepped forward and knelt.

"My Lady Mariota," he said and his voice held sadness and respect. "Here are those whom you asked to see. They came willingly and travelled with gladness. They are truly your folk. They are like the yeast to a tub of malt!"

The woman at the door nodded.

"Come, Hilda." Her clear command rang like a bell across the glade. Murdo stood aside and watched his wife gather her skirts and run over the springy grass to her mistress.

Mariota turned and disappeared inside. Mac Eth rose to his feet. "Now you shall meet the other one in my lady's household." With the hound at his heels he strode towards the small kirk. Murdo followed. The sun, balanced on the rim of the ocean, trailed a fishnet of shining herring across the sky. In the valley, its silver rays transmuted moss to emerald, rose-berries to rubies and wild-cherry leaves into medallions of polished bronze. Mac Eth, Murdo and the dog Lulach approached the cross. Small shadows on its ancient stone, sharpened by dusk, revealed the interlacing plait and mysterious animals, half reptile, half beast.

In contrast, the tiny church was built of plain black slate with a turfed roof. Beyond it, a small herd of milkers and their horned steers grazed where the brambles gave way to myrtle and willow.

"You have a fine place here, Mac Eth," said Murdo and felt embarrassed by the sound of his voice, for the silence in that tiny strath, buried in the womb of the mountains, made speech an intrusion.

"Too much for two men's hands and scarce enough for three, though Gillanders has kept it tidy enough on his lone," was the grudging reply.

They doffed caps and entered the church through its single arched door. Candles glowed and flickered beneath the Crucifixion, and sunbeams, streaming through a rose-window on the west wall, touched the back of a man in white who knelt at His feet. In that small place, empty except for the life-size statue, whether by trick of light or by the nature of his build, his long back, broad shoulders, and spade-like hands clasped in prayer, were those of a giant. In contrast, the round shaven head that bent and bobbed as he read from the Scriptures looked ill placed and incongruous. His voice too was unexpectedly soft, and high-pitched.

Such was the commanding effect of this piece of heaven amongst the high mountains that Murdo knelt down at the door of the kirk and joined Gillanders in his praise to God the Giver. "Who shall ascend into the hill of the Lord – or who shall stand in his holy place? He that hath clean hands, and a pure heart; who hath not lifted up his soul unto vanity, nor sworn deceitfully. Who is the King of Glory; The Lord strong and mighty, the Lord mighty in battle. Lift up your heads, 0 ye gates; even lift them up, ye everlasting doors; and the King of glory shall come in." All three men were on their knees. The preacher moved. There was a quiet rustle and he was on his feet facing the two worshippers. "Son of Eth, welcome home," he said. "And Murdo McInnes too, welcome. I perceive an upright man and a contrite heart. Pax vobiscum."

Thirty-four

Murdo and Hilda spent three years at Applecross with Gillanders and Mariota de Athyn. For Murdo, it was hard and welcome work, calving the beasts, turning the earth with the cas-chron, the "twisted foot" that a man can use on his own to plough the narrow strips of ground between mountain granite and burn. In season, he carried panniers heavy with rotting seaweed to spread on the used soil, scythed, stacked, hand-threshed the corn and ground it to meal in the little mill he built by a waterfall. Neither Gillanders nor Mariota touched flesh, but there were fish aplenty in the sea-loch and shellfish in the shallows. Milk, butter, kail and corn, cheese, both goat and cow, provided variety and abundance they shared with the village children who came to help and to learn and who stayed to eat.

Hilda brushed out the tangles in her mistress's long silvery silken hair and listened. Her talk was sometimes gay and trivial, often heart-wrung, anguished and laden with guilt. Gradually, as the months passed, Mariota learned to live with her past, a past she had shared with the man whom the Church had dubbed "the wickedest man in Christendom", a past she had convinced herself was wholly reprehensible in the eyes of God. But as she confessed her guilt to Hilda her fears became less frightening, her sins just a little less Satanic, her prospects of resurrection more hopeful.

But what a strange tale it was that she unburdened on her erstwhile serving-woman; a tale of ceaseless searching after redemption and forgiveness, of self-imposed penance, of guilts real or imagined that lay upon her like the Cross of Jesus. She called herself a murderess and described how at the age of six she had pulled the heads off her dolls before making her escape from her father's castle. She remembered how near she had come to suffocating her youngest son, Andrew, as he lay gasping and burning with fever, possessed, she believed, by the Devil whose touch she so feared. She blamed herself for the death of the earl, who had been sacrificed, she said, because of her adultery with a priest. That was what she most regretted, her temptation, to satisfy carnal lusts, and the flaunting of her wickedness in the face of the Wolf, the one man she had deeply loved and yet betrayed.

But there was one other confession imprisoned in her heart and when, at last, she unlocked that secret the darkest sins of her troubled soul came stumbling into the light. They came amid a frenzy of tears and groanings, when she tore her hair and drove her nails into her face until it bled. The tormented ramblings were at first meaningless to Hilda, but with repetition and coaxing, the story became coherent, and shocking. "When I planned my shameful seduction of Philip Hogeston I little knew I was but compounding a felony for the church of God! I knew that the frightening scene, created by the Wolf during that last supper in Lochindorb, was designed to hide from all but myself and the monk our true crime. At night, when the Earl came to my room, he nearly killed me. The pity 'tis he did not unleash all his anger on me then, and end my life!

"Days later, shut away in my prison-house in Buchan, my lover, Philip Hogeston, arrived. Lover no more! He upbraided me for a deceitful liar and a scheming whore, who had plotted with the Wolf to have him burned at the stake for crimes he was guiltless of! In his rage, he blurted out the true reason for his incarceration at Lochindorb.

"It was a tale which, at first, I refused to believe. He told me that it had been the Bishop's personal, confidential command to him to gain entry to Lochindorb and to cuckold the Wolf! Thus did Alexander Bur seek to break the bond between my lord and me, a bond which he considered an offence to the King and to the Church, but chiefly against himself. If Philip Hogeston had not been captured at the firing of the Cathedral, some other way would have been found to insinuate him into the lair of the Wolf! He admitted that the greatest risk he had been obliged to take was at the Cathedral gates when he was surrounded by the Wolf's men. He had been surprised by his luck. He could have been hacked to pieces!

"So it was out! Far from being the designing female, from the first time I set eyes on Philip Hogeston, I was the victim of an evil plan by a Bishop of God's Holy Church to get rid of me, by using the sins of lust, fornication and deceitfulness as his weapons! With these unholy tools he slammed the wedge of suspicion and lost-love between myself and Alexander Stewart. No doubt he enjoyed his joke when he proclaimed that Evil had been overthrown by the wrath of God! The wrath of God indeed! Profanity, witchcraft of an odious kind and, certainly, the weak flesh of a woman had all been enlisted by that unscrupulous bishop!

"And what did that make me? The instrument of the Devil? I know only this for sure. By betraying the Wolf, I broke the spirit of a wilful and unforgiving man who glimpsed the meaning of God's love for His people, which is beyond the nature of the greedy and selfish clergy to understand!" Bishop John Winchester had quoted those final paragraphs in heavy, large, script and, to reinforce their importance, he had underlined them. Was this what Bishop John Winchester himself believed? Batchelor of Common Law, Bishop of Moray in fourteen thirty-seven, the same year that saw the murder of his King, he occupied a position of power at a period in Scottish history when the Monarchy and the Church dared not slacken their grip on the Realm, against the press of anarchy, heresy and the predatory English.

Now that he at last knew the truth about how Alexander Stewart, Wolf of Badenoch, had been "reclaimed" by the Church was it any wonder that he had buried this dangerous knowledge under a hundredweight of Caithness slate! Mariota poured out her secret thoughts and her fears to Hilda McDonnell and told her of her wanderings from holy shrine to holy shrine in search of absolution until, at last, exhausted, weary of life, she was led by her kinsman Mac Eth to this haven of Applecross, to become the acolyte of Gillanders the Culdee.

It took a long time and much woeful repetition, with encouragement from Hilda, before the poor, distraught, devil-ridden woman could bring herself to lie prostrate on the cold slabs of the church and tell all to her Redeemer, in the sole presence of her confessor, the saintly Gillanders. Her confession lasted several days and during all of it she lay on the kirk floor in a long shift of uncarded wool through which she had woven nettle-stems and heather-roots. This cruel self-imposed atonement blistered and cut her soft white skin which Hilda washed each night with loving care. She had eaten nothing for weeks. Only her determination to confess kept her alive.

Thirty-five

Mariota did not fall ill – she despised such weakness in herself – but one morning, only a few days after the ordeal of her confession, she said to Hilda, "My hour is nigh."

Ever since Murdo and Hilda had arrived in Applecross, Mariota had been haunted by the nearness of death. "Should I die today, what will happen to my poor soul?" she would say. "I don't want to wander endlessly across the deserts of purgatory. I want to see the sweet goodness of this world slowly fading, as the stars rush out for me. I want to see the Far Islands beneath my feet and hear the cry of the seabirds in my ears, and then no more."

It was a bright blue day in February. "My hour has come," she said. "My load of guilt lies now in the little church. Its floor is ankle-deep in the dung of my sins!"

The stream chuckled and splashed in a spirited spate which plunged from the snow-corries to the lazy sea; a pair of dippers sang their love-song to each other as they bobbed and whirred from waterfall to waterfall. Mariota watched them. "I am going to walk to the village, but by myself," she said to Hilda. "I want to speak with the father and mother of Angus McFee and persuade them to give the boy to God's Holy Church. He is an angel, and must become a monk. They have many sons, those two, who can work the boat and look after them in their old age!" She brushed Hilda's protestations aside. "Before I go," she said, "I want to enjoy my own company and the friendship of God's creatures this crystal morning."

When she did not come back, Murdo, Mac Eth and Gillanders set out to find her. She had spent some time, as she had said she would, with the McFees, but had left them at midday. The morning had been calm with a high fan of pale cloud and the air so clear that the homes of the Raasay folk, although leagues across the Sound, could be counted by the white reek of their fires. But, as the short day died, a cliff of black cloud advanced on Applecross and dark came early with a whipping of sea-foam and a sting of hail.

During that long wild night the men searched, calling, calling. McFee and two of his lads joined them and they lit fires, with difficulty in that gale, so that, like a moth lost in the night, she might see and come to them. Then the hard cutting hailstones turned to sleet and snow and the men knew they were beaten.

All the village turned out next morning, to search for "The Lady". The sun flashed coldly from a moving sky, the wind had dropped and snowflakes fell listlessly on the new, white world. Their search continued, all fearing what they might find, men and women, scanning the shore and the snow hummocks in the wood, with eyes that expected what their lips would not say.

Mac Eth and Gillanders clambered up the frozen hillside to the Pass, probing drifts with poles, alert for the softer feel of a creature, living or dead. The snow was crisp and the wind bundled it into shapes that spread from the lee of the rocks like ermine tails. Near the summit there is a flat place – like a giant's chair, from where, on a clear day, the faraway Hebrides can be seen, smoke-blue against a sapphire sea. There, on the edge, where the cliffs plunge down to the village of Toscaig, a stiff snow flag streamed from a white hump that should not have been there. Mac Eth broke away the snow feathers and found her, wrapped in her cloak, frozen, like all else in that lifeless landscape. The two men gently freed her body of ice. Her little prayer book they left clasped in her rigid grip.

Gillanders said, "Leave her be. She has carried that little book with her, as she carried it through life."

They buried Mariota near the ancient cross of the Pict people, that looks out over the bay to the vast sea-space of the ocean and which rises like a sword or, as Gillanders described it, the finger of God.

Mac Eth, the tough gypsy from Erin's Isle, kneeled when he had lowered her into earth's cold clasp, and his tears splashed on her grave, tears which neither Hilda's calm acceptance nor Gillander's assurances of her place in Heaven could assuage. The last of her lovers, he mourned her going with the keen sorrow of his own loss.

Hilda and Murdo said farewell and turned their eyes beyond the Pass of the Beast to distant Badenoch.

Gillanders retreated to his little church and sought remembrance, or forgetfulness, of his last true convert in the lofty love-song of King Solomon.

Mac Eth dug out a weeping willow, catkin-soft, from its adventurous hold by a rocky pool and planted it in the new-turned soil. There it drooped silver tear-drops above the grave, where lay the mortal remains of his beloved Mariota, mistress of Kings, mother of Knights, widow of the Wolf of Badenoch, but to him queen of the land of dreams, his Tir nan Og.

Epilogue

Five centuries later, I stand on that same "giant's chair" below the Pass of the Beast. Ben Alligin and Ben Liathach hump their ancient sandstone cliffs high above Loch Torridon and to the northwest I see the Far Islands as Mariota must have seen them, smoke-blue smudges on a sapphire sea. And I ask myself the questions that plagued Bishop John Winchester, whose bones have rested this half-millennium in his tomb among the ruins of Elgin Cathedral. Mariota could not have spoken an untruth in her confession. Did she then confess to God all that she had told to Hilda McDonnell? If she did, there is an answer to the "Bishop's Riddle". If she did not, then,

Wha slew the Wolf and his whelp of Garth
Adultery, witchcraft or God's Own Wrath?

Historical Notes

The Wolf of Badenoch and Mariota de Athyn.
  Alexander Stewart, a son of King Robert II of Scotland, made himself infamous in history by his destruction by fire of the Cathedral of Elgin in 1390.
  Mariota de Athyn, his mistress, bore his family of five sons and one daughter. It is the part that she played in the fortunes of her sinister man, 'tragedian without equal' in Scotland's turbulent history, that this story tells.

Regent Robbie – The year 1363, the year that followed a murderous epidemic of the "Black Death", found Scotland in the turmoil of Civil War. King David II, whose first wife was sister to King Edward III of England, by secret diplomacy with his brother-in-law nearly succeeded in reversing the triumphs of his father Robert the Bruce. If he had had his way he would have sold his kingdom to the English crown and Edward's son Lionel might have ruled Scotland! Although David himself survived to continue his undistinguished reign, the plot to destroy Scotland's independence was bloodily squashed by the Wolf's father, "Regent Robbie", who later succeeded to the throne as King Robert II.

Devorgilla Balliol, daughter of Alan of Galloway and Margaret of Huntingdon, married John Balliol of Barnard Castle and Picardy. Their son, also John, became King for a disastrous four years that ended in the conquest of Scotland by Edward I of England (Hammer of the Scots) in 1296. The marriage of Devorgilla and John is one of the most moving love-stories of

Scotland's Golden Age. After his death, she confirmed and endowed the college in Oxford University that bears his name, and which he had founded, under "stress of penance." Devorgilla herself "founded in Galloway an abbey of the Cistercian Order: Dulce Cor she made them call it, that is Sweet Heart. In her abbey, she lies buried, the embalmed heart of her husband worn close to her breast, in a casket of silver and ivory." (Andrew de Wyntoun 1390).

Seath Mor of Clan Kay – That accomplished swordsman's son Seath-beg, or Shaw the younger, takes his place in Scottish history as the leader of Clan Kay in a gladiatorial fight on the North Inch of Perth. There, at the command of King Robert III, the Wolf of Badenoch's half-brother, thirty warriors from Clan Chattan (Macpherson) fought an equal number of Clan Kay to settle a matter of honour. In the presence of the Royal Court, that fierce battle raged until the last remaining swordsman of Clan Kay was confronted by eleven Macphersons, all wounded, but alive.

Lochindorb and Loch-an-Eilean – Situated between Carrbridge and Forres, and south-west of Aviemore, respectively, these two island fortresses of the Wolf of Badenoch differ in many respects. The former is a gaunt castle in a bleak, featureless loch. The other is a fairy-tale fortalice built on a small island in one of the loveliest glens in all Scotland. To the thoughtful visitor, the contrast between these two lairs of "The Wolf" is so striking as to suggest that the man who occupied them was a more complex human being than the plain brute that his contemporaries persuade us to see.

Ruthven and the Standing Stones of Easter Kingussie – The A9 Highway from Perth to Inverness sweeps boldly into Badenoch through the Pass of Drumochter and crosses the river Spey at Kingussie. In the spring, vehicles, roofed with coloured skis, speed on towards Aviemore, their occupants uplifted by the sight of Carn Ban Mor and the crags of Coire Guisachan, white against a blue sky. Few will drop their gaze and the sharp roofless gable-ends of Ruthven Barracks on Castlehill pass unseen. So too do the twin knolls at the centre of Kingussie where stand Columba's graveyard and the old presbyterian manse. Yet those three landmarks, important to this tale, glitter with past glory. The Barracks speak of rebellious years between "Glencoe", and "Culloden", when the redcoats of the House of Hanover tramped the Highlands on General Wade's new roads; when Ruthven was like a red spider in the centre of its web. Centuries before, a castle stood on the hill, a fortified palace for the Wolf of Badenoch. His Justiciar's Court was at the Standing or Standard Stones of Easter Kingussie, more than likely, on the knoll of "Columba's graveyard". And three thousand years before that, men had raised their stone circle for a purpose which eludes our understanding.

Bishop Bur's Petition – "In Dei nomine amen. Robertus Dei Gratia Rex Scottorum. Humillima mei recommendatione permissa... I beseech your assistance in rebuilding my cathedral, which was the special ornament of our fatherland, the glory of the kingdom, the delight of strangers, the praise, and exaltation of praise, in foreign lands..." So runs the petition of Alexander Bur, Bishop of Moray to King Robert III of Scotland, following the burning by the Wolf of Badenoch of the Cathedral at Elgin on seventeenth of June 1390.

The Lang or Bishop's Steps, connected the island of Duffus, its castle and the Hogeston estate of Plewlands (now Gordonstoun School) with the mainland north of Elgin and provided a ford over the narrow western channel of Spynie loch, then ten times as large as it is today. A succession of expensive, and therefore litigious, drainage projects have released hundreds of acres of arable land and even the stone pillars of the "Steps" have vanished. Now the prosperous farms of Crosslots and Waterton sit on what was, until two hundred years ago, black loch-bottom under six feet of brine, and clam-shells upheaved by the ditchers are there to prove it. (The Wolf).

James Stewart and Janet Menzies – In accord with custom, a child-marriage was arranged between James Stewart, a son of the Wolf and Mariota, and Janet Menzies of the Appin of Dull. In the settlement, the justiciar secured the pass between the extreme south of his territories and the lush lands of Strath Tay and Glen Lyon. Above the perpetual roar of the Kelty gorge, the Wolf built Castle Garth, the future home of the young couple. Ever since it rose, crag-like, from the heather, it was a reminder of the long arm of the Lord of Badenoch. James Stewart, when he came of age, lived up to the reputation of his terrible father and is known in history as "The Accursed Whelp". (Blood of the Wolf).

The French Knights – "The Auld Alliance" between Scotland and France promised mutual aid and, in time of national peril, help, which was readily given throughout five centuries, against "The Auld Enemy", England. In the year 1385 Scotland was invaded by the army of King Richard II commanded by John of Gaunt. The English possessions in France had been reduced to a handful of channel ports and, before mounting a continental offensive, Richard had to secure his northern border. So, by force and bribery, he secured a truce with King Robert. The French thought this was a cowardly evasion of the Alliance and, to put spirit into their allies, Admiral Jean de Vienne landed in Scotland in May with a substantial force of horse, knights, men-at-arms, 50,000 gold francs and armour, to revitalize the Scottish resistance. Linked under the common banner of St Andrew, the allied force laid waste northern England as far as Newcastle, but the results were certainly not worth the punishment meted out by King Richard. In massive retaliatory expeditions, he burned Dryborough, Melrose, Newbattle and Edinburgh. The French knights left when winter came, disgusted with their quarters, the weather and the conduct of the war. They condemned the Scots guerrillas as unchivalrous, their policy of scorched earth as wasteful. The Scots found their allies quite unbearable and were glad to see the back of them!

Cover Design: The Digital Canvas Company
                  Forres
                  Scotland
                  bookcovers@digican.co.uk

Layout: Stephen M.L. Young
                  stephenmlyoung@aol.com

Font: Adobe Garamond (11pt)

Copies of this book can be ordered via the Internet:

                  www.librario.com

or from:

                  Librario Publishing Ltd
                  Brough House
                  Milton Brodie
                  Kinloss
                  Moray IV36 2UA
                  Tel /Fax No 01343 850 617